General Editor: Aidan Chambers

THE DAY OF THE PIGEONS

Mousy Lawson runs away from Approved School one
Friday evening. He is determined to find his father who
has just written saying he has married again and is
leaving the country. Mousy gets a lift in a lorry, reaches
London, finds an empty basement in which to live, and
starts looking for his father. That's when Chris enters
Mousy's life, in search of Monsieur Poirot's prize
pigeons.

Chris thought Mousy nothing but a nasty little thief and
a dirty fighter, but he is unwillingly dragged into Mousy's
search and before long he is not sure what to do about
Mousy – or Mousy's criminal father.

Roy Brown is a teacher in a school for handicapped
children as well as the author of many stories for
children and teenagers. Two of his books, *A Saturday in
Pudney* and *The Day of the Pigeons,* have been filmed.
Another, *The Viaduct*, has been dramatised for television.
Other popular stories are *Flight of Sparrows* and *Bolt Hole.*
All his books are published by Abelard-Schuman.

drawings by James Hunt

The Day of the Pigeons

Roy Brown

Macmillan Education
London and Basingstoke

First published in Great Britain by Abelard-Schuman 1968

First published in *M Books* 1979
Reprinted 1983, 1984

Published by
MACMILLAN EDUCATION LIMITED
Houndmills Basingstoke Hampshire RG21 2XS
and London
Associated companies in Delhi Dublin
Hong Kong Johannesburg Lagos Melbourne
New York Singapore and Tokyo

Printed in Shen Zhen, China

ISBN 0 333 25715 4

Contents

1 Journey by Night

Mousy Lawson absconded just after sunset on the Friday evening. It was not especially difficult – the Approved School was no prison, only a large country house converted for the purpose. There was always an interval between Supper and Dormitory when, as Mousy had noticed, everybody seemed to slacken their vigilance. The heavy door at the end of the wide hallway was still unlocked. On the other side, at the foot of a flight of broad, stone steps, the drive began its curve between beds of thick shrubs.

Mousy avoided the gate, with its lodge. He turned off the drive half-way along, cut through the shrubs and picked up his packed haversack where he'd hidden it a few hours ago; then he climbed the wall dividing the grounds from a steep, quiet road. There was a chance that someone at a high window might spot a climber, but it was getting dusk and Mousy was nimble.

He dropped into the road, crouched and listened. There was no sound of alarm or pursuit, only the smooth purr of traffic far down the hill on the main road from Bristol to London. He adjusted the haversack straps on his shoulder and walked on, not too quickly, not too slowly. He reckoned he had at least half an hour's start before the panic started and he was missed: when, probably, old Potter checked up in the dormitory. It should take less time than that to reach the drivers' café – the one called STAN'S PULL-IN (hot dogs; egg and chips 20p). Mousy had spotted the place a few weeks back on returning from a coach outing. It was bang on the London road.

Mousy met no one on the hill. Before long it was quite dark except for the twinkle of vehicle lights between the trees on his left. The road was soon close. Easy, so far! Mousy grinned to himself wondering, cockily, why he had stayed at the School all that time – over a year. But he knew the answer: it was no use running away unless you had somewhere to go. Other kids had tried it and been picked up within a few hours. You had to have a plan. Mousy had a plan.

When the hill joined the road he quickened his pace, keeping close to the hedgerow on his right. Telephone wires twanged overhead. Several vehicles passed in both directions, cutting swathes of brilliance across the highway, sometimes blinding – seeming to Mousy as suspicious and inquiring as policemen's torches. He had to make himself walk casually, even when he wanted to dive into the hedge, as though he were a local lad on his way home from a club. He was glad when he spotted the neon sign over the café – red for STAN'S PULL-IN, green for HOT DOGS and the rest. Only the 'H' tube was defunct, so the sign flashed on and off nervously: 'OT DOGS, 'OT DOGS.

Mousy got up close to the wire fence marking off the vehicle park. The café windows were opaque with smoke and steam. The smell of fried food came tantalizingly from the oasis of yellow light. The café was probably not crowded yet – it was too early. Only seven or eight lorries waited outside.

Mousy looked them over, keeping well back in the shadows. It was a fair bet that the trucks facing east were, in fact, in the process of travelling to London – or in that direction. He *could* be lucky and get there in one jump; but the important thing was to make a start. Mousy paid special attention to the sides of the cabs. The firms owning the trucks usually printed their addresses there.

One lorry hadn't an address – or was so covered with dust that it couldn't be read in the dim light. A second, and a third, bore the names of towns Mousy had scarcely heard of. Then as he peered through the fence at the fourth his pulse quickened: H. E. TIMMS & SON, IMPORTERS, PERRY STREET, LONDON S.W.8.

Wasn't *that* a district not far from Victoria Station? Near enough – Mousy was sure of it. The lorry belonged to a firm in

South West London, and the chances were it was on its way home. Mousy knew he wouldn't get a better 'break' than this, and at any moment the driver might come out of the café.

He ran back to the edge of the fence, near the road, and got the lorry between himself and the café windows. It was a massive vehicle almost the size of a removals van – so much the better, safer to stow away in. Mousy climbed up on the spare-tyre rack at the rear, clung to the tailboard and tried to see through the heavy canvas curtains. A dry, sour odour came out of the darkness. He set to work on the knot of rope securing the two edges of canvas, poked his head through the gap, then drew his legs in behind him.

He had just retied the knot when voices sounded outside. A man laughed. A door slammed. Feet crunched closer, but nobody came round to the back of the truck. A moment later the vehicle rocked slightly, its engine throbbed to life and they were lurching across the parking space into the road. Mousy waited by the tailboard, taking a peep to make sure they had turned in the right direction, then crawled cautiously forward.

This was a stroke of luck all right! Mousy groped, found a space on the floor to sit on, took a torch from his haversack and shone the beam in the freight. Piles of sacks made cliffs all around him. He'd crawled into a cave between the cliffs. Some spillings, and the smell, told him that the sacks contained flour. Presumably the load had been picked up at the Bristol docks. There were some loose sacks at the front and Mousy set to work to make himself a bed of sorts. The August evening was chilly, but it was going to be snug enough in here. Mousy, who had roughed it much worse than this in his time, wrapped another sack round his shoulders and leaned back, listening to the truck's wheels settling down to a steady throb on the open road.

He switched off his torch, but it wasn't quite dark. Between the halves of the canvas curtain he could see the moon rolling along behind them like a silver plate. Then he closed his eyes and thought things over.

His skipping off like this was going to surprise them up at the School. They wouldn't have been expecting it. They thought Mousy Lawson was contented enough which, until the letter had arrived, he had been. The school was well run and equipped, had a kindly and humane staff and, although there were a few bullies there they had tended to leave Mousy alone. The other boys had liked him, though they called him 'crafty' and 'deep'. He had arrived with an enviable reputation as a bold and incorrigible thief. He had tended to keep himself aloof, and he'd been only wryly and good-naturedly rebellious. Why should he abscond? Where would he go?

On drummed the wheels. The truck was no express, but it was fast enough. Sometimes, the chink between the curtains flared white as a faster vehicle drew up behind them: a police car, maybe? Don't be stupid, thought Mousy. This isn't the telly! He unbuckled his haversack again, and switching on his torch went through his belongings, carefully collected together during the week. There was an old road map torn from a school atlas, showing the road from the west ending in a pool of pink representing London; a pair of clean socks, neatly rolled; a bar of chocolate beginning to go soft; a packet of stale corned-beef sandwiches filched from the canteen the previous evening. And, at the bottom, still in its envelope, the letter from his father.

Mousy munched some of the chocolate, took the sheet of paper out of the envelope and read it through. There was a date, but no address on the top of the letter.

Dear Keith,

Sorry I haven't written for ages, but I've been busy. This is just a line to say a temporary good-bye, son. If a certain little prospect pays off I reckon to leave the country – for good. It'll be good-bye to the old life.

I know you've sometimes said you wanted us to be together again, just like the old days. But it can't be done now, Keith — not while you're at that school. Just be a good boy and later on we'll fix things so that you can join me in the new country.

By the way, you've got a stepmother. That'll surprise you! Her name's Audrey. She's one reason why I've decided to settle down and make a fresh start. We've been living at the old house while things are working out, but not for long, if all goes well.

There's no need to write back. I'll let you know, somehow, where we land up, and when. Don't talk to anybody about this letter, in case what I've told you gets around. There's a big job in the offing, and the less certain people know about that the better.

Your loving
Dad.

It had taken Mousy some time to plough through the letter when he'd first received it. He wasn't a great reader and his father's handwriting was hasty and ill-formed. It had taken him even longer to make up his mind what to do.

In some ways the letter was puzzling. During the week Mousy had done a lot of guessing about parts of it. Once or twice he had wakened at night, tossing and turning with doubts, questions, longings, fears.

The big flour lorry trundled on. Mousy felt the sacks creak against their securing ropes as the truck was negotiated through a roundabout junction. The driver changed gear and on they went. London, here we come!

He refolded the letter and took an old snapshot from his pocket. It was one of several he'd kept through the years. His brow furrowed in the torchlight as he studied it — for the twentieth time that week.

It showed a house — a pretty ordinary sort of house with a tree in the front garden. There was a gate, and on the gate post there was a number — 17. Two figures stood beside the gate.

One was a much smaller, younger version of Mousy. The other, a burly, unsmiling man, was his father, Ted Lawson. They stood staring into the camera, hand in hand.

Mousy had been about seven, then. Now he was over thirteen. This was the 'old house' his dad had mentioned in the letter. Six years was a long time and Mousy cursed at the tricks memory played. He could remember so many things, but not the name of the street where the house had stood. He thought, vaguely, that it had borne a queer, foreign name – and there was some sort of field or park along one side of it. This was more a feeling, though, than a memory.

Mousy had racked his brains all week. Why hadn't his dad troubled to write the address on the letter? Mousy hadn't been able to think of any way of locating the house without alerting the School authorities . . .

Except one: go to London himself and find it. That's what he would do, he'd decided. He'd skip, get to London, find the house, give his dad a big surprise! So his dad thought he couldn't take Mousy with him, because he was at Approved School?

'Don't you believe it, mate!' he murmured into the darkness. 'I'm on my way.'

Mousy ate one of his stale sandwiches. He felt thirsty. He wished he'd 'nicked' a flask of tea. He wished he'd brought some smokes.

What would he call this new stepmother? Aunt Audrey?

He fell asleep.

He awoke with a start. The truck seemed to have grown wings. It was practically flying along, its big wheels whirring like dynamos. Mousy nearly panicked. He scrambled back to the tailboard and peered out into a grey, wet morning. At first he was afraid lest, during the night, they had taken an unexpected, divergent route. But then, from signs and hoardings, Mousy knew that they were at the approaches to the capital. He went back, buckled his haversack, and waited – and waited.

At last he reckoned they'd come far enough. As soon as the lorry slowed at a set of traffic lights, Mousy stuck a leg over the tailboard and baled out. A motorist hooted at him as he landed bang in front, but he darted away and got clear into a side street.

Rain still drizzled down. Mousy slipped into a shop doorway and caught sight of his own reflection in the window. What a mess! He must, he realized, have got himself smothered with flour from the sacks in the truck. Why hadn't he thought of that? A few moments in the wet had turned him into a freak – something made of *papier maché*.

Mousy swore. He hated getting himself in a mess. More serious, he knew that he daren't be seen in public in such a state. It would invite suspicion. He was conspicuous enough as it was, with his stuck-out ears, pointed face, blond hair; with the flour paste to draw attention to him, any rozzer, once his description was circulated, would be down on him in a flash.

He would have to clean himself up before attempting anything else. The rain was teeming down, now. Where could he clean up? He couldn't see a 'gents'. Passers-by were already giving him curious stares.

Mousy dodged away – away from traffic, away from faces. He began looking for somewhere to hole up. He must get off the streets – and quickly.

His quest brought him into the district of Pimlico. The buildings did not offer any immediate sanctuary, being mostly large blocks of flats, workshops, garages and commercial buildings. Mousy was really looking for a rubbish dump. Mousy didn't mind rubbish dumps. Once, in Bristol, he had lived for a week in a hut made of old tyres and corrugated sheeting.

Gradually the streets widened out and sometimes there were short cul-de-sacs which acted as the service roads to houses which had once been elegant: they had flat roofs like fake balconies – and basements. Mousy blinked through the rain; were those basements inhabited? He approached one on a corner and peered down a flight of broken stone steps. Below, a single smeary window with two panes missing gave access to a dark, bundle-filled room.

There were curtains at the windows above, but not down there. Mousy took a chance on being seen and crept down the steps on to the area of cracked concrete. Cautiously he picked the sharp bits of glass out of the window frames and wriggled through.

Not bad. The place was filthy, of course. The basement was cluttered with broken furniture and what seemed like sacks of old rags. But a pool of daylight on the far side intrigued him and when he groped towards its source he found that the basement, on the other side of a smashed, partially boarded up doorway, let into a small, walled garden. It was at a level, surely, lower than the streets on the other side of the walls. Rain pelted and dripped out there, and Mousy ignored the garden for the time being. He cleared himself a space between the rag bundles and squatted down in the dry.

So far, so good – things might have been a lot worse. Here was shelter, and he had found it before getting quite wet through. Here was a place in which to think out his next move. Presently he would tackle this flour paste on his clothes and in his hair. Then he would make a first try at finding the house. That might take time. His hurried, rain-soaked journey from the lorry had not given him a chance to get his bearings.

He would need a map – a street map. He might find the street marked on it, and remember its name. And food, and some means of cleaning his clothes. He couldn't stay skulking down here for ever. But it was early morning, yet. He would dry off a bit, then, when the shops were open, he could go on 'the nick', so long as he was careful not to get caught. That would be too bad, running straight into a copper and being sent back to Bristol – what a waste that would be!

Something moved by the garden door. Startled, Mousy whipped round. But it was only a cat, coming in from the soaking garden. It was a huge, black cat with fur matted in the rain and grey whiskers and filmy-green eyes. It looked half-starved.

The cat stared at Mousy in the detached, incurious manner of its kind. But when Mousy offered it some corned-beef it wandered nearer and took the tit-bit out of his fingers. Then, instead of going away, it curled up stiffly beside him and set to work washing its tangled fur.

Mousy listened, wondering if the cat belonged to somebody in the house above and whether they would call it in. But nothing happened.

After a while the rain stopped abruptly and sunshine lighted the cracked, dusty pane of glass in the door. In a way, it was like footlights being switched on for the second scene of Mousy Lawson's adventure . . .

Act Two. Pimlico, London, Saturday . . . But Mousy wasn't having any such thoughts. He was only thinking, 'As soon as it starts drying up a bit, I'm going on "the nick". Then I'm going to find my dad.'

2　The Pimlico Pilferer

P.C. Angus Dickie's spell of duty ended at two that week. His beat covered several blocks of the quiet backwater of Pimlico and no one would say that his duties were either exciting or onerous. In fact, in the constable's own opinion, there just could not be another part of the great city of London so law-abiding and downright dull.

The Scots policeman knew very well that this was as it should be, of course. He would have been the last to recommend the introduction of gangsterdom, robbery with violence, or any of the crimes he sometimes watched being committed on his landlady's TV. On the other hand, since his great ambition was to become a detective, he sometimes wondered how on earth this was to be achieved when he never met a real crook from one week's end to another.

Angus was well aware that before you got into the C.I.D. you had to show initiative, preferably attracting the notice of someone high up at Scotland Yard. Passing examinations was only part of the process. It helped a lot if you obtained information leading to the arrest of a notorious criminal, or flung yourself in the immediate path of a jewel robber's fleeing car.

Nothing like this ever happened in Pimlico. The friendly, sleepy inhabitants had never, apparently, heard of jewel thieves and wouldn't have dreamed of harbouring dangerous international bandits. And what made Angus particularly disgruntled was that his landlady's son, Bert Trunket, *was* a detective constable; *and* he was attached to Scotland Yard.

What, Angus was wondering that Saturday morning as he plied his beat through the busy shopping area, did Bert Trunket have that he didn't have? Luck, of course. Och! that was all there was to it – luck. Well, mostly.

He morosely examined a couple of cars that had been parked in a certain spot too long, but not quite long enough for it to be illegal, then sauntered at regulation pace along the big fence enclosing the Maybe Site. Big Annie, the crane, leaned against the sky like a metal giraffe. Below, the building site lay deserted and unworked like an abandoned diamond mine. It was called the Maybe Site by the locals because, they said, some day there may be a new building completed there and maybe not! Some of the building *was* there. You could see the scaffolding for miles; or you could if other, older buildings weren't in the way.

Labour troubles had stopped work, off and on, for several years. And financial troubles, and troubles caused, it was said, by quarrels amongst sinister and distant people called speculators.

Next to the Maybe Site was a block of august, elderly buildings including an insurance office, a barracks (no longer housing soldiers, but a-clack with typewriters) and a couple of banks. On night duty, Angus had the job of keeping an eye on such places and trying the doors. But he had never found any unlocked, much less jemmied, and in any case as he well knew they were practically seething with stalwart watchmen and burly representatives of *Securicor*.

Then came the underground station which marked the limits

of Angus's beat. Here he crossed the thoroughfare, strode along Petty France, then turned left along a street lined with various small shops. And it was here, at Mr Burridge's the ironmonger's, that he got his first chance that day of using what those Scotland Yard high-ups might have called 'initiative'. Big deal! Mr Burridge had left several price-reduced lawn mowers inelegantly spread out across the pavement in everybody's way.

'Causing an obstruction, aren't ye?' said Angus.

The ironmonger, a bald, short, irritable man glanced up reproachfully. He said, 'You coppers make me laugh!' (But he wasn't doing anything of the sort.) 'When you're wanted you're nowhere to be found. When it's too late, along you trot grousing about obstructions.'

'Hold on!' said Angus, worriedly. 'When did you want me?'

'Oh, hours ago. What are we supposed to do – blow a whistle? Some kid came through here like a mini-crime-wave. Whipped no end of stuff – no end. Nobody could catch him.'

A small group of hostile shopkeepers assembled round Angus. The greengrocer said, 'I managed to grab his shirt, but he tugged clear. Helped himself to some of my apples – Granny Smiths.'

'He pinched a tin of cat food from me,' said the grocer. 'And two packets of biscuits – assorted.'

'I rather think some cigarettes are missing,' said kindly Miss Patchett, more in sorrow than in anger. 'But he looked too young to smoke.'

'Some of 'em smoke in their cradles,' commented the greengrocer. 'Anyway, he wasn't all *that* young.'

'You got a guid look at him?' inquired Angus.

'Just a back view, when he nearly lost his shirt.'

'Only quite a *little* boy, I thought,' said Miss Patchett.

'Fair hair,' added the grocer. 'And there was some muck on

his clothes – something white. Chalk, maybe. I always keep a few boxes of matches on my counter. He just slipped in through the door, grabbed some matches and scarpered.'

'Matches?' frowned Angus.

'Well, naturally,' sneered the ironmonger. 'He'd want matches to light his fags with, wouldn't he?' Angus felt annoyed at his sarky tone. He'd better watch it, had Mister-blooming-Burridge.

'Pity your door was open,' he said, mildly.

'Well, it's hot, isn't it, after the rain? You can't blame me because . . .'

'And what did he take of yours, Mr Hollis?' Mr Hollis kept the draper's shop on the corner.

'I was his last pitch, so to speak. Funny thing, this. He stole a perfectly ordinary clothes brush. What can a youngster like that have wanted with a clothes brush?'

'To brush the chalk off his clothes, of course!' suggested the grocer.

'Do little boys care about that?' asked Miss Patchett.

'He *wasn't* little,' protested the greengrocer. 'Not all that. I got a side view of his face when I grabbed his shirt. It was an old wizened sort of face, if you know what I mean. Old, and wizened . . .'

'I bet he's hiding somewhere – somewhere with a lot of chalk about,' said the grocer.

'How did he carry all the stuff?' asked Angus. 'Never in his pockets!'

'Not likely,' chortled the ironmonger, ironically. 'He did it in style. He pinched a carrier bag off the nail right here, by my shop door, then collected the other loot as he went along – bang, bang, bang. And where,' he added, with a grand gesture of his arms, 'was the law at the time? Watching the changing of the guard?'

Angus reddened and turned away. He stuffed his little black

notebook back in his tunic pocket. That, he was thinking, was the public for you. Och! they expected you to be in a dozen places at once. They thought you had as many arms as an octopus.

He had better try and get a lead on this youngster. Where had he come from? Was he a local laddie? And why that queer mixture of stolen items; apples, sweets, cigarettes, matches, a clothes brush – and a tin of cat's meat!

He strode on down towards the old flats. Some children were playing by some dustbins outside. Children liked Angus, and he liked them, too – unless they were cheeky and rash enough to call him 'Dickie Bird' or make 'tweet-tweet' noises behind his back.

He questioned the children. He questioned most people he met. Nothing. On the way back he thought of chalk. The grocer had claimed the laddie had had chalk on his clothes. Where in Pimlico was there a lot of chalk? At the Maybe Site, of course.

Big Annie loomed above the scaffolding, agleam in the sun. Angus tried to peep over the fence. He was tall, yet he could not see much – just parts of the deserted site; trenches, concrete footings, pieces of excavating machinery. Near the fence, behind a solid locked gate, was a long, timber office building. Angus had occasionally seen workmen go in and out of the gate. Were any of them in there now, and had they caught a glimpse of a fair-haired boy dodging about in those excavations? Kids did climb the fence, sometimes. It was dangerous, and illegal, but they did it. And apparently this laddie didn't care much for keeping to the rules. But the gate was locked; there was no sign of life.

Angus continued his inquiries with diminishing hope. Whoever the boy was, no doubt he had left the district by now. To have stayed would have been asking to get caught.

Far across the park, Big Ben struck the quarter hour. Angus

23

thought about Mrs Trunket's lemon meringue pie as he returned to make his report. Then he fetched his bicycle from the car park at the back of the police station and rode thoughtfully home with his arm band stuffed into his tunic pocket.

Mrs Trunket ran a small newsagent's and tobacconist's off Victoria Street. Her son, Bert Trunket the C.I.D. man, wasn't at home today. Angus greeted Mrs Trunket cheerfully, using lots of broad bogus Scots which usually amused his landlady. 'Och! away, then, an' I'm starved, woman. Weer's me wee slice o' lemon pie?'

Mrs Trunket, in the shop, wasn't at all amused. 'Burnt,' she said.

'What's that?'

'The whole dinner burnt to a cinder while I was off down the street chasing the young hoodlum who robbed the shop.'

'WHAT'S THAT?'

'Not half an hour ago,' said Mrs Trunket, her voice shaky. 'I'm still trying to get my breath. A fair-haired boy with stuck-out ears. Chalk on his clothes, too. I couldn't catch him. He ran off towards the hospital. I was going to phone the police, but . . . well, he didn't take money, or anything much.'

'What did he take?'

'A street map from the counter rack. Perhaps a few sweets. I had the door open, because of the heat, so the bell didn't ring, of course. I heard a scuffle, went into the shop and there he was – just the back of him.'

Of course, it must have been the same thief – the Pimlico Pilferer. Angus was inclined to the dramatic. He saw dramatic headlines in his head, if he wasn't careful.

PIMLICO PILFERER STILL AT LARGE

Well, *that* was true, at least. If he had been chased by Mrs Trunket, then it meant he had not left the district.

Mrs Trunket, her face flushed, seemed to attach some blame to Angus, not that she exactly said so. 'Pity you didn't happen to be home. What kept you – a spot of traffic trouble?'

Angus let that pass. 'You sure that's all he took – a map? Some sweets, maybe?'

'And the *Daily Express*.'

'You didn't say that at first.'

'Does it matter? I just remembered. I'm sure there was a single copy of the *Daily Express* on the counter.'

'If only I'd been back a wee bit sooner,' said Angus, and he was about to explain. 'You see . . .'

'Well, you couldn't be everywhere,' said Mrs Trunket, magnanimously. 'That nipper would've had a shock if he'd known two policemen lived here. Wait till I tell my Bert! My Bert would've given him what for.'

Bert, the detective; Bert-blooming-Trunket of Scotland Yard! Angus, his pride wounded beyond endurance, muttered, 'I'll have him.' Then he added an uncouth phrase he'd never even heard in bonnie Scotland. 'Och! I'll have his guts for garters!'

He didn't mean Bert Trunket, of course. He meant the Pimlico Pilferer.

After his morning forays, Mousy lay low throughout the afternoon – in fact he didn't go out again all that day. Too many people had seen him. Once he had been chased nearly all the way back to the basement; his hideout might have been blown. He'd bungled things a bit. He'd been in too much of a hurry, much too careless and cocky. He'd have to watch it from now on.

The day turned out stiflingly hot. Outside in the walled garden steam rose from a tangle of weeds and long-forgotten vegetables which twisted themselves into odd, personal shapes like mutations of snakes. Mousy sat out there in the sun, trying to brush and pick off the flakes of hardened flour.

There were steps leading up to a small railed landing and door belonging to the dwelling above. The door never opened. Nobody came down into the garden. Apart from the buzz of wakened insects, all was silence.

Mousy used a brick and a nail to hack open the tin of cat's meat, fed his companion, ate some of his stolen biscuits and drank from a bottle of orange squash. (The grocer hadn't missed that!) When they had finished, and the cat prowled off after birds, Mousy studied the newspaper. He didn't find any reference to himself – he hadn't really expected to. Who did he think he was – Al Capone? The street map wasn't of much use, either. It covered too big an area, the print in the index was too small to read, and there seemed to be a lot of streets with foreign-sounding names.

But he located the position of his basement all right; it was about a mile from Victoria Station. How was he to begin to search for the house? It was too late to do much more today – and he didn't want to venture out of hiding again for the time being. Perhaps tomorrow he could think of some way of getting hold of a better map, or a street directory . . . but tomorrow was Sunday. It wouldn't be easy. Nothing would be easy on Sunday.

Mousy felt confused. He took another look at the snapshot, read his dad's mysterious letter again, trying to guess what it all meant. Then he impatiently stuffed them away, lit a cigarette, and smoked thoughtfully, waving his hand to and fro between puffs to scatter the smoke and not let it be seen above the wall.

There was a lot of time to kill. But when twilight came at last he made up a bed just inside the broken door of the basement. He did not touch those bundles of rags, though. There would be lice in them. Mousy had got lice more than once, and he hadn't forgotten. He took off his jacket and tucked it round his shoulders then lay down close to the wall. It was sheltered enough down there.

Night came. The strokes of Big Ben counted the hours. Mice scuttled in the basement and sometimes Mousy saw the green, shining eyes of the cat on the prowl. Once he heard a voice in the room above: a soft plaintive twitter, as though someone were addressing a sick canary. There was the whisper of slippers on the floor. Mousy slept fitfully.

Over the newsagent's, so did Angus Dickie. He dreamed of a fair-haired boy with a 'wizened' look. The boy was running, running along an alley with tall walls of chalk. 'I'll get ye!' yelled Angus, in his dream. 'Tweet, tweet!' said the boy, and put his fingers to his nose. Angus woke in a sweat.

'I'll get him,' he told the darkness. 'If he's about tomorrow, I'll have him!'

But tomorrow was another day. Tomorrow was the day of the pigeons.

3 Open the Traps!

'My boys and girls' as Mrs Trunket called them, finished their paper rounds by about nine o'clock on Sundays. On this Sunday the first one back waited for the last, because Bruce Roper had said, 'After the round on Sunday I'll show you Monsieur Poirot's pigeons.' And Bruce Roper was last back.

When they had given in their satchels, five of them cycled away from the newsagent's until they reached one of the flat-roofed terraces between Victoria Street and the Maybe Site. The five bicycles were left leaning at the foot of the stone steps leading up to the roofs, their handlebars twisted together in frozen attitudes of conflict like the horns of thin, quarrelsome cattle.

The pigeon lofts were arranged high up round the edges of the small roof area. They were built securely on stout frames of timber and at one end was the store where the foodstuffs and various equipment were kept. The door of this place was half open, and faint, breathy whistling sounds came from inside.

'Well, here they are,' said Bruce Roper. 'Sidney's given them their breakfast. In a minute we'll toss 'em.'

'Toss'm?' said Beverley Bright. 'And where's Sidney?'

'Tossing means setting the pigeons free,' explained Bruce. 'They come back of course. They're trained. They fly round and round in whacking great circles, then they come back. I've tossed them dozens of times. They don't half go! Sidney's in the shed.'

Sidney was Bruce's little brother and he had just learned to whistle. The Ropers lived almost next door to Monsieur Poirot, the Belgian pigeon fancier, as people called him, though he had lived right here in Pimlico for thirty-five years. While Bruce had gone on his paper round, Sidney had been left in charge of the lofts.

Bruce inspected the lofts, checking that the hoppers were full of grain, giving the gang a guided tour and some expert instruction. Bruce was fat, so he puffed a good deal when he climbed up and down the frame supports. He showed them the traps which were hinged in such a manner that the homing pigeons could re-enter the loft but not get out again unless you wanted.

And the different nest boxes, carefully divided from one another, each occupied by different kinds of pigeons. Some were old and some were young. Pigeons weren't just pigeons; there were dozens of different kinds, Bruce said: albinos, gay pieds, cobbies, chequered pigeons. 'I've even given the racers names,' he grinned, shyly. 'Just the six in this loft. They're the ones I'm going to toss in a minute.'

He told them the names he had given them. They weren't Monsieur Poirot's names, of course, just Bruce's. The two albinos were Oswald and Egbert; David was a cobbie, Henry a chequered pigeon; Pigeon George and Pigeon Freddy were gay pieds.

Chris Barker, the eldest of Mrs Trunket's boys, frowned because he knew just a bit about pigeons. He didn't think much of giving six beautiful, highly-trained racing birds ordinary and facetious everyday names, as if they were parrots or puppies.

And he was wondering something. 'I thought pigeon fanciers concentrated on *one* strain of pigeon,' he said. 'This Monsieur Poirot has all sorts.'

'Yeah, well,' said Bruce, 'I think he just *likes* pigeons. He doesn't put them in races, much. He just breeds them, and *likes* them – all kinds.'

Leo Chan, Mrs Trunket's half Chinese boy, wanted to know what kinds of pigeons were in the lofts on the far side of the roof. Bruce hadn't said much about them.

'They're just old pigeons and young pigeons, and sick pigeons. In season Monsieur Poirot breeds his squabs and squeakers in those lofts. And some of the sick pigeons have one-eyed cold or foul feathers. Or they're wrongly-bred, like being long legged . . .'

'Why doesn't he wring their necks?' asked Chris. He had never been cruel to a bird in his life, but he wanted the gang to know that *he* knew about pigeon fancying. He knew that pigeon fanciers sometimes wrung the necks of useless pigeons because it was a waste of food and time to keep them. That was if they cared more about racing than they did about pigeons.

'Cor, Monsieur Poirot wouldn't do that,' said Bruce, his friendly, plump features horror-stricken. 'I told you – he *likes* pigeons. He thinks they all have a right to live, even if they aren't much good at racing or winning prizes at shows.'

Lena Chan, Leo's twin sister, understood. She and Beverley Bright crossed to the other lofts to look at the useless pigeons. In the store shed, Sidney went on whistling and clattering. Nobody took any notice, yet.

Bruce explained about pot eggs, blood quills, strags, hackle feathers; the importance of keeping the lofts clean because otherwise you got mites. Mites were a menace. And food. Food was important for pigeons. You couldn't feed pigeons on scraps. That would be asking for trouble.

'And you're looking after the lofts for a fortnight?' asked Chris Barker, enviously.

'Yes, Monsieur Poirot's gone on his holidays. He's still got relations in Belgium, see? Well, I usually come and help on Saturdays, so he said I could mind the pigeons for the whole fortnight. He's paying me, too. Now, this is how you work the traps . . .'

He was nearly ready. The girls came back. Everyone stared through the chicken wire into the racing loft. Bruce stared, too. Far, far at the back of his mind something was worrying him. He didn't know what – yet. For the moment he was remembering one of Monsieur Poirot's little jokes. 'I do not think I could wr-ring their necks, Br-ruce. Though I do not mind r-ringing their feet.'

Bruce told the others another of Monsieur Poirot's jokes. It was really a riddle. 'Do you know why chickens don't go to Heaven? Well, because they have their necks whirled in this.' He looked disappointedly at their blank faces. 'Necks whirled, *next world*. Get it?'

Beverly Bright giggled. The Chan's faces were round and shiny and smiling. Even Chris Barker grinned. Then there was one of those silences that come by accident. The soft murmurs of the city came gently across the roof-tops. The morning dew was steaming off the slates and sunshine caught the wings of the ringed pigeons, brightening the bloom of their feathers. The albinos looked pink.

But all six pigeons seemed so drowsy and uneager . . . Bruce's elusive worry crept nearer. Yesterday, when Bruce and Sidney had tossed the pigeons, they had stood wide-eyed as the feathery creatures had fluttered and cooed, then burst out of the opened traps and gone swooping over the roofs like kites in a gale . . .

That was it . . . today they *weren't* cooing, they weren't excited.

'Go on then,' said Beverley, impatiently.

'We'll just fetch Sidney, first,' said Bruce, and his mouth felt dry.

Beverley was the first at the store. She called out, 'Oh, come and look at Sidney!'

Bruce reached the shed door. 'Oh, brilliant!' he said. 'What's been going on Sid?'

'Look what I done, Brucie,' said Sidney, proudly.

Sidney was six and a bit. He wasn't fat like Bruce, but his hair was normally just as dark, his face usually just as round and pink. But today Sidney looked like a picture in a horror comic. From top to toe he was smothered.

The store contained jars and receptacles of all kinds, each carefully labelled and occupying its own space on one of the shelves. Tic beans, codliver oil, grit, hempseed, tares, maize corn, green food – and, placed on the other side of the shed, several bags of chemical fertilizer. It happened that Madame Poirot grew plants in pots, and she shared the store with Monsieur Poirot. One of the shelves had collapsed and Sidney, squatting on the floor, had managed to get practically everything into one huge disgusting heap. He was scooping bits of the heap with a little metal shovel and tipping it into one of the jars.

'Sidney, that's naughty,' said Beverley. Beverley had a motherly streak.

Bruce hadn't. 'Leave him to me,' said Bruce. There was a special way of talking to Sidney, just as there was a special shell for penetrating an armoured tank. 'Look, did you get any of that fertilizer muck mixed with pigeon food? You know I put the mixture ready for you, and told you how to put it in the hoppers? Well, *did* you?'

Sidney scraped some hempseed oil out of his hair and grinned back with a mouth decorated with something that looked like potassium cyanide. 'Dunno,' he said, cheerfully. 'I *give* 'em their breakfast, Brucie.' He seemed to sense that this explanation wasn't quite what Bruce wanted, so he added, 'The shelf fell down.'

Bruce went crimson. 'You stupid little twit! *Did* you feed any of that muck to the pigeons?'

'That's what he's done, you know,' said Chris. 'I bet that's what he's blooming done.'

'Oh, brilliant!' said Bruce.

They hurried back to the loft. Bruce clambered heavily up to take a closer look at the hoppers. No, it didn't look right; there was a damp, clogged look about the contents of the hoppers. The pigeons were pecking half-heartedly at the mixture.

'What's supposed to be there?' asked Chris.

'Maple peas, maize – all sorts.'

'I bet there's all sorts in it all right! It'd take a laboratory test to find out just what. Are you going to let them go just the same?'

'Yeah, well . . . what's the difference? They'll either fly out or drop dead.'

'If you let them out,' said Leo Chan, 'at least they won't have a chance to eat any more from the hoppers. You can wash them out before they come back. We'll all help.'

'Here goes, then,' said Bruce, and he jerked the cords of the traps.

One by one the pigeons dithered out of the loft. Pigeon Oswald, an albino, gyrated his wings enthusiastically. Then, as if his wings were made of lead, he fluttered across to the peak of a roof opposite and perched there shaking himself. Pigeon David, the cobbie, came out next, followed by Pigeon Henry, the chequered. They both made a few crazy swoops and loops over the street before tail-spinning down and waddling through gaps in fences.

Pigeon George and Pigeon Freddy, the gay pieds, stood on the edge of the trap like reluctant pirates walking the plank.

Their wings gave a clockwork twirl or so, then they flopped dazedly on to the roof and waddled off under the sick quarters. Beverley and Lena Chan hunted for them, but they had gone, as if melted by the sun.

Pigeon Egbert, the other albino, was last away. That one was shrinking in a corner of the loft, his head buried in his feathers. The protruding beak showed a speck of corn stuck in his mandibles. Chris climbed up and ventured nearer and nearer like a bomb disposal expert approaching an unexploded charge. Pigeon Egbert blinked one red eye, cooed, opened his wings and made a rush for it.

'There he goes!' yelled Beverley. They watched him until he had fluttered two streets away, vanishing behind a tall office building.

There was a long silence. Somewhere in the distance, church bells pealed. Traffic hooted along the main streets. A boat wailed on the river.

Chris said. 'They're gonners. They're half poisoned.'

'Do pigeons migrate?' inquired Beverley, senselessly. Then she added, hurriedly: 'I mean, if they fly somewhere they may work the poison out of their systems, then they'll come back. *Swallows* come back.'

'Oh, shut up!' said Bruce. 'Who's talking about swallows? What's Monsieur Poirot going to say? I'm going to *kill* Sidney.'

Leo Chan said, thoughtfully, 'Look, we've all seen how dazed they are. That means they aren't likely to get far. Suppose we go straight after them, catch them, and bring them back? *Some* of them anyway.'

Lena Chan nodded. She had been thinking almost the same thing as her twin brother. She nearly always did. 'Some will be better than none,' she said. 'I wouldn't mind helping.'

'Neither would I,' said Beverley.

'I'll have a bash,' said Chris.

Bruce cheered up. 'Okay, thanks.'

'What are we going to carry them in?' asked Beverley.

'We'll have a look round,' said Bruce.

There were some pigeon transporting baskets next to the store, but they were too big for carrying on bicycles. Bruce collected Sidney and they all went along to the Ropers' garden. Bruce said there was a lot of useful junk there.

Chris bagged an old tool box which had a hinged lid and was empty save for a few cobwebs which he blew away. There were sufficient breathing holes where the handles had been fixed, and he could tie the box securely on to his carrier.

Leo was lucky. He tripped over a bird-cage which was hidden amongst the weeds at the top of the garden. The Ropers' deceased budgerigar had lived in it. It was a big cage. One of its rusty sides slipped completely out of metal grooves, so it would not be necessary to push a pigeon through the proper spring door.

'It's even got a bell,' laughed Lena Chan. 'And a perch, and a seed bowl.'

'We'll take the perch out,' said Leo. 'More room.'

Beverley Bright wasn't so lucky. She wondered about a flower pot. There were some large red flower-pots lying about, but most of them were broken. In any case they would be difficult to carry. Then she found a saucepan, and that had a handle. It was a big, brown-enamel saucepan and a little extra rummaging around produced the tin lid to go with it.

'No air holes,' frowned Chris, disapprovingly.

'Oh, yes it has,' said Beverley, triumphantly, and she showed him the bottom of the saucepan, which was simply laced with holes where the rust had worn it thin.

After this they trooped back to Monsieur Poirot's lofts. Bruce issued them each with a twist of paper containing a little un-adulterated pigeon mixture. They could feed the pigeons with it – maybe even use it to tempt the shy ones.

'When you grab them,' he said, 'don't squeeze too tight. Sidney and I will stay up here for a while because of cats. The cats are always hanging about licking their chops. And if they spot any half-poisoned pigeons creeping back . . .' He didn't finish. He left everybody to use their imaginations.

Chris tucked the tool box under his arm. 'Here we go, then. Wish us luck.'

Bruce laughed uneasily. 'We're all going to need it. If Monsieur Poirot comes home and finds his racing pigeons gonners . . .' He didn't bother to finish this sentence, either.

Off they went. Pimlico was awake, now. It had awakened so slowly, bit by bit, without any of its weekday urgency and bustle. Church bells pealed, then stopped. Traffic snored. The streets lay empty and clean, like the blue, washed sky.

On the roof next door a couple of cats appeared, one ginger, one a tabby. The tips of their tongues were pink and their eyes were icy bright with anticipation. Bruce fetched a bean pole. He put it in Sidney's sticky hands. Then they waited.

4 Boy in Hiding

Leo and Lena Chan, riding their bicycles, carried the bird cage in turn. The cage had a convenient little ring at the top which you could hook a finger through. They hadn't far to go – only to the Chinese Restaurant, in Pimlico. They looked out for pigeons on the way but had no luck.

'There are all sorts of pigeons about,' said Leo. 'Wild pigeons, mostly. Perhaps Monsieur Poirot's pigeons have got mixed up with *them* by now.'

'That's what *I* was thinking,' nodded Lena Chan. 'In the park, or across in Trafalgar Square – perhaps even at Buckingham Palace.'

Leo laughed, then he said, 'We'll fetch Jimmy and Heather. They're old enough to be sensible.'

Lena smiled. 'I was just going to say, let's take Heather and Jimmy because they're sensible!'

They often made a joke of the way they thought of the same things at the same moment. It happened time and time again. People said it was because they were twins.

At the restaurant they collected Jimmy and Heather Chan, Jimmy was eight and Heather was seven. Jimmy had a round, placid face like Leo's. Heather's was more pear shaped. Although Lena's face was like Leo's, it *was* a little pear shaped.

They set out on foot, Jimmy Chan carrying the bird cage. They hadn't gone far when they saw Beverley Bright talking to Angus.

'There's Beverley,' said Leo, 'talking to Dickie Bird.'

It wasn't cheeky, the way Leo said it. It was quite respectful. Leo Chan was always respectful, even when he referred to Angus by his nickname.

Beverley Bright cycled carefully and wobblily home. She wobbled because of the saucepan, of course. She had thought of strapping it to her carrier, but tying something big and round to something small and oblong was more difficult than it sounds – especially if you didn't have any string.

So she simply balanced the round part of the saucepan on the steering shaft of her handlebar and let the long handle rest in her lap, or held it between her knees. Either way was uncomfortable. Every time her legs went up and down on the pedals the saucepan rocked and rattled and nearly slid off.

She was solemn and thoughtful on the way – and hot, too. It was a hot, awkward ride because of the saucepan and the weather. Even in the shade between the tall buildings it was hot. She thrust her squarish face forward determinedly. Her pony tail swished untidily behind her. Suddenly she thought of Bruce's joke about the chickens who got their necks whirled, and that made the handlebars wobble worse and she nearly fell off.

When she got home her mother asked, 'Where are you going now?'

Beverley was coming, not going. But she told her mother about the pigeons and her mother said, 'They won't come back, you know. The other birds will get them. Tame birds never survive in the wild. Look at canaries. You're not taking Connie on that old bike.'

'In the wild,' giggled Beverley. 'Oh, mummy, London isn't the jungle. This is Pimlico, not Papua!'

'I'm beginning to wonder,' said Mrs Bright, hotly.

'Are we going to see the ducks?' asked Connie.

'No, pigeons. Have you washed?'

'Coo!'

Connie was five and the thing about being five was that if Beverley had said they were going to look at boa-constrictors or alligators, that square little face would have carried the same blank, matter-of-fact expression.

Beverley had left the saucepan on the front step. She let Connie carry the lid. They ran most of the way through the baking streets until Angus's helmet popped up from behind a wall like a giant blue beetle.

'What have you got in that saucepan?' asked the policeman, coming into view. Beverley explained. The Chans arrived, and they explained, too. Angus nodded. He said, 'I've got a hunt on, also. Maybe you can help, while you're looking for the doos.' He told them about the thefts the previous morning. He knew they were some of Mrs Trunket's boys and girls.

'Mrs Trunket told us – a little,' said Beverley. 'Is that right you call him the "Pimlico Pilferer"? . . . Do you think he's still about?'

'Could be,' said Angus. 'It's a hunch I have. The trouble is we don't know much about him. Some say he was only a wee lad, and some say different. But we do know he's fair-haired and yesterday, at any rate, he had chalk on his clothes.'

'What do we do if we catch him, Mr Dickie?' asked Leo, seriously.

'Arrest him on the spot,' grinned Angus. He liked to be jolly whenever he could. 'You want to borrow my handcuffs?' But it was really no joking matter. He straightened his face. 'Weel, good luck with the doos, anyway.' He waved and walked off.

'*Doos?*' said Lena. 'What are doos?'

'Pigeons, I suppose,' said Leo. '*Scotch* pigeons.'

They walked along together a little way.

'Isn't it hot?' said Lena.

'No wind,' said Beverley. 'Look, the weathercock on top of the church isn't moving.'

They all glanced up at the church spire. Faintly behind the stained-glass windows across the churchyard came the soft strains of organ music. Leo stopped dead. 'It *is* moving. Look, it's flapping its wings!'

They suddenly remembered that there wasn't a weathercock on the spire of this particular church. The bird up there was a real live bird – a pigeon!

It seemed to overhear them discussing it and fluttered from the spire across the churchyard, across the street, alighting heavily on a high window ledge of one of the office buildings. Then it began using window ledges as stairs, partly hopping and partly flying down and down until they saw its colouring clearly. It was one of the gay pieds. For an instant, the hot sun's rays caught the ring on its foot. Then it was right down on the pavement ahead of the children, shaking its feathers like bed-clothes. It was only thirty or forty yards away.

'Come on!' cried Beverley, and she was the first after the pigeon. She held the saucepan out in front of her and Connie came after, waving the lid. The pigeon seemed to know it was being chased. It set off along the pavement, waddling fran-tically, making no further attempts to fly. Mostly its head jerked to and fro with the rapid movements of its legs; but sometimes it turned round and peered behind it, or stopped altogether and pecked stupidly at the pavement.

Beverley soon caught up. She put the saucepan down on the pavement. It made a dull, short sound like a cracked bell. She put out a warning hand behind her, making the others approach more carefully. She was so close to the pigeon, now; she didn't want it to be startled afresh.

The pigeon stood against the wall of a building. It was Pigeon George – one of the two pieds. Pigeon George looked at her through his red-bead eyes; he watched her outstretched fingers, fascinated, his beak opening and shutting. Little bubbles of saliva gleamed on the points of his beak.

Then suddenly, watched by the rest, Beverley leaned forward from her crouched position, and grabbed with both hands. She felt the plump, warm, oily pigeon in her hands. She dug in her fingers too hard and the pigeon, thinking it was about to have its neck whirled, struggled to get free and cawed madly like a rook. Pigeon George was a warm, oily, slippery some-

thing in her hands, but Beverley made herself hold on. 'Connie
... the lid ... ready!'

Connie was ready. Trying not to look at those scared, ruby
eyes, Beverley pushed Pigeon George into the saucepan. There
was plenty of room. Connie banged the lid down – much too
hard. Pigeon George must have been deafened! But he was
in.

Lena asked. 'Wouldn't he be more comfortable in our
cage?'

'And who caught him, may I ask?' demanded Beverley –
haughtily, greedily.

'You did,' smiled Leo. 'It's okay. Lena was only wondering.'

'I'm taking it back to Bruce,' persisted Beverley.

'Okay, okay,' smiled Leo. You never could quarrel with Leo
Chan. 'Well, be seeing you. We're off to the park.'

Beverley and Connie watched the Chans go towards St
James's Park. Beverley picked up the saucepan. The saucepan
lid gave an eerie little jump and rattled. The saucepan felt very
heavy. The pigeon might have been carved out of stone.

'Please may I peep?' asked Connie Bright.

'No,' said Beverley. She still felt greedy. 'There's room for
another pigeon in the saucepan. Let's see if we can find *another*
pigeon.'

At the foot of the roof steps, Chris Barker fetched his bicycle, hesitated as he wheeled it across the pavement, then set
out towards the hospital. He had seen Beverley wobble off in
the other direction – the Chans, too. There was no point in
them all hunting in the same area.

Besides, Chris didn't mind being on his own – at least some
of the time. Later, if the pigeons were rounded up, he would
call for a couple of his school chums and they'd go fishing,
maybe. Right down as far as Putney they'd go. It was going to

be a hot day, but Chris didn't mind that, either. He loved the open air, and the heat, and being on his own, or being with his chums, and fishing. He liked being free and busy and on the move.

He could smell the dust coming off the roadway under his tyres. Down among the old houses and yards, across Victoria Street, gates were padlocked, windows curtained or shuttered.

It was a hot, dusty, deserted area. He kept his eyes skinned but saw no pigeons, only a few cats.

He caught sight of one particular cat sitting by some railings. Behind the railings some steps led down into the basement of a house – one of a terraced row.

The cat was watching something; its back was arched, its fangs bared, and it was crawling stealthily towards the steps. And there, pecking at the top steps was an albino pigeon!

Chris slithered to a standstill, parting from his bicycle in a single agile leap, letting the machine clatter over where it met the kerbstone. His onrush startled the black cat out of its wits. It drew back its ears, flicked its tail and scampered off along the pavement. The pigeon stopped its aimless pecking and hopped sparrow-like down the basement steps. When Chris reached the steps it had vanished, but he'd seen the ring on its foot.

Chris went down the steps, ignoring the curtained windows above. The pigeon had vanished – it must have fluttered through the shattered window. Watchful for glass fragments, Chris clambered through. After the blinding sun glare of the street he found himself in almost pitch darkness. Then, without warning, a hand grabbed him by the throat.

He was taken right off balance, swung sideways, then down on a dark, dirt floor. He felt his arms being pinned beside him, held down by two hands that gripped like twin vices. A knee was planted in his solar plexus. Fighting for breath, Chris dimly made out the faint blob of a face above him.

'If I let you go, are you going to do anything stupid, mate?' The voice was squeaky and panting. Chris painfully shook his head. Reluctantly and gradually the steely bands loosened their grip and the knee slid away.

Chris staggered to his feet, ashamed and humiliated. He'd always thought himself stronger than average; but this kid . . . crumbs! He was a tiger.

Chris could see, now, that his assailant was a boy not much older than himself, though slighter. He had fair hair, a pointed face, protruding ears and eyes that seemed to burn. 'Are you on your tod? Nobody out there, waiting?'

Chris badly wanted to rub his sore arms, but he didn't. 'Have a good guess – *mate*.' He was nearly a foot taller than this kid. He should have been able to pin his ears back for him – but he didn't try that on!

The boy swore. 'Don't give me none of that,' he drawled.

'I'll bust your flaming nose! What are you doing sneaking down here?'

Chris never got round to explaining. He didn't even know if the boy had seen the pigeon. Chris wasn't thinking about pigeons any more. He suddenly knew who the boy was: he was the kid who'd stolen the things from Mrs Trunket's shop. He half turned to dart for the window, but the boy grabbed him with a hand like spring-wire. 'You're not going anywhere, mate. Come outside where I can see you properly, and keep your mouth shut.'

Chris obeyed. He wasn't afraid of the boy. No, it wasn't that – exactly. He was more fascinated than frightened, as though he had wandered into a patch of weeds and trodden on a snake.

Out in the garden they both crouched out of view of the upper windows and there was a long, appraising look between them. The boy's ferocity seemed spent, now. There was still that wild look in his eyes, but he seemed uncertain what to do next.

Chris felt better out here in the sunshine. After all, he had the fugitive, one way or another. What could the boy do to stop him running off for the law, the moment he chose? He might try more of his tough stuff, but Chris reckoned he could cope with that in the open. Just now the boy had had him at a disadvantage. Chris said, quietly. 'I know about you. You should have had more sense, sticking around. Why didn't you stay on the move?'

'What do you know about me, exactly?'

'You've been pinching things. I know you're trying to dodge the police. You're not a local kid. For all I know, there might even be a reward for your capture!'

Unexpectedly the boy grinned. 'The trouble with you, mate, is you read too many story books. You go to the police and they'll pat you on the back and say, "Well done, you good little citizen." If that's what you want, push off and collect.'

Chris stayed where he was.

The boy said, tauntingly, 'What are you waiting for? Afraid I'll trip you up on the way out?'

Chris got to his feet, then. 'I'm going, don't you worry. I suppose you'll be gone when we get back, but you won't get far. I passed a copper just now, right on the corner.'

That was a lie. Chris had seen nothing of the sort. He just wanted to shake this sudden cockiness and bravado. The boy was making no attempt to stop him. Why not? Did he think Chris *wouldn't* fetch the police? What gave him that idea?

Chris turned for the basement, half expecting the boy to make a dive for his legs. Instead, the squeaky voice said, 'Before you go grassing, you don't happen to have anything to eat on you? I'd go out and nick some, only the shops are closed on Sundays.'

Chris went – and the boy didn't stop him.

Mousy could hear his own heart thudding. He was playing this close to the wind, trying a colossal bluff. Sharp-witted, used to being in tight corners, Mousy thought he'd seen hesitation in the kid's face. He was no softy, but he was curious. A lot of those kinds of kids were curious about you. In a way, they even wanted to be *like* you. They even started off by being on your side. Mousy had learned this from experience.

That kid hadn't just met a rozzer; he'd fibbed about that. And he was curious. He'd make some excuse to come back, then he'd ask a lot of questions. That was what they always did, those kids.

Well, not *always*. Sometimes they got scared, then they went whining to the rozzers. Sometimes they shopped you in the end. Perhaps that kid would do that. Perhaps Mousy ought to have a bit of sense and skip from here before it was too late.

But it might not be easy to find another hideout as good as

this one. He *had* to stay around until he had found his dad. He wasn't running again if he could help it.

Mousy lit a cigarette and leaned back nonchalantly against the wall. But his heart still thumped. Would the kid come back with the rozzers? Maybe. He'd just have to wait and see. If that happened, he could always skim over the wall and try a get-away.

5 Street of the Little Pig

It was after ten o'clock when Chris left the basement. He picked his bicycle out of the gutter. The handlebars were hot to his touch. He mounted the machine and rode away slowly, drifting in and out against the kerb.

He thought over what had happened. It had all been so sudden. He'd gone down those steps after the albino pigeon and the boy had jumped him; a filthy, hunted-looking boy with white muck on his clothes. A hungry boy.

Then there had been a fight – if you could call it a fight. The boy had acted tough and talked tough. Then he'd seemed to back down a bit, maybe because he'd known he was nabbed and couldn't do much about it. In a queer sort of way he had more or less dared Chris to fetch the police – as if he wouldn't!

He was a thief, the thief who had robbed Mrs Trunket. A widow robber! A mean, nasty little 'hood' who stole and was hiding from the law. Spiteful, too. Chris could still feel a dull ache in his middle where the nasty little 'hood' had knelt on him.

Chris began pedalling faster, though he didn't notice. He was making himself furious with these memories, all this hate for the unknown fugitive. Fetch the police? Not half, *mate!* I'll fetch the police all right. The first policeman I meet, I'll tell. 'Before you go grassing, you don't happen to have anything to eat on you?' That's what the boy had said. So what? He practically deserved to starve, didn't he? Served him right!

Chris had a sudden thought. Suppose the boy hopped it before Chris got back with a policeman. He probably would. Had he believed that bit about Chris's meeting a copper on the corner? And suppose he took the policeman to the basement and the boy wasn't there any more. A right Charlie Chris would look then, wouldn't he? It would be better, thought Chris, if he went back to the basement on his own first – found out more about the boy, if he could. What could he tell a policemen if the boy hopped it? Crumbs, he didn't even know his name!

Almost without realizing it, Chris found the bicycle taking him home. He knew his mother was out, but he had a key. He let himself into the flat. In the kitchen, the breakfast things were draining next to the sink. Chris didn't touch them; it would be better if his mother didn't know he'd called indoors.

He set about making up some sandwiches. Bread was no problem because two cut loaves had been opened and a few slices from each wouldn't be missed. To avoid raiding the fillings too much he mixed the sandwiches – one of meat paste, one cheese, another full round of beef extract. He hoped the fugitive's tastes were varied! When he had wrapped the sandwiches he added a wedge of ginger cake and put the lot in a brown paper bag. He found an empty medicine bottle, rinsed it under a tap and filled it with milk, corking it securely.

That should do. Chris cleared up the crumbs, put everything away tidily and left the flat. He put the food into the tool box on his carrier and rode away. At the first corner he met Angus! Chris would have nodded and ridden past – quickly. But the constable was waving him down, so he had to stop.

'Any luck with the doos?' He looked at the tool box!

'Doos? Oh . . . no, not yet.'

'I was telling the others, about keeping an eye open for the thief. It's just a wee idea I have, that he's still abroad. I may be wrong. Laddie with fair hair and chalk in his clothes . . . did Mrs Trunket tell you?'

'Yeah,' said Chris, and rode on. Too quickly? He felt Dickie Bird's eyes on his back.

Chris left his bike along the street a little way. He scowled at the curtained windows and crept down the steps with his paper bag. The boy was squatting in the same place, but his careless indifference didn't fool Chris. He must have been watching his lone arrival down the steps, then hurried back. He was picking at his clothes. 'You didn't bring the cavalry then?'

There was a taunting look on his filthy face. Chris flung him the bag of food. The boy said nothing, only grinned. Then he tore the wrappings away, snatched a sandwich and sank his teeth into it. He was half-way through the third before he noticed the cat rubbing his leg. He gave it a crust, offering the bag to Chris, who shook his head.

'How long do you reckon you can stay here, then?' asked Chris. He was annoyed because the boy didn't ask why he hadn't fetched the police. If the fugitive cared one way or the other he was taking jolly good care not to let it show! Chris went on, 'I just met a copper I know. I really did this time. He's got it in for you, because it was your fault his dinner got burnt.' Mrs Trunket had told them that bit! 'As a matter of fact, *two* coppers live over the shop you raided. I'm not kidding. And *one* of them's a Scotland Yard bogey.' Chris knew that crooks called detectives 'bogeys'. He also wanted the boy to know that he'd just talked to a policeman, but hadn't grassed.

The boy's eyes gleamed oddly and he grinned. 'Go on? You reckon they'll have a patrol car out looking for me, yet?'

But the funny thing was that he was being half serious. The

possibility seemed to excite him and his dirty face was almost triumphant. Chris saw this and thought: he's like a little kid lighting a bonfire, watching the flames, half hoping to get his fingers burnt. Who was he? Where had he come from? What was he hiding down here for, apart from dodging the police? Why hadn't he kept moving?

Mousy uncorked the medicine bottle and drank from it in one long draught until drops ran down his chin making thin, white rivulets in the grime. Then he let the cat lick the neck of the bottle and threw it aside. He'd eaten all the food by now; hogged the lot in a couple of minutes. 'Ta, mate,' he said at last. 'That was very civil of you.'

'Don't they feed you – where you live?' asked Chris.

'Now you're fishing, eh? You want to know where I've come from. Well, I'll tell you, mate. I'm from Bristol way, and I bust out of an Approved School.' Apparently he expected applause for that. 'I had my reasons, but they're none of your business.'

But Chris guessed a bit of it then. He said, 'You're looking for somewhere, aren't you? You stole a street map from Mrs Trunket!'

'Very clever,' mocked the boy. His mood changed subtly. He was thinking something over. Then he glared at Chris, hostility suddenly resumed. 'What are you waiting for? Feeding time's over.'

Chris looked angrily back. 'Don't get the idea I'm helping you any more. I need my brains tested for not calling the cops in the first place.'

The boy looked nasty. 'I'm not asking any favours from you, bonzo. Fetch the rozzers and be done with it. But don't be surprised if one of these dark nights you get a knife in your ribs.'

'Don't you threaten me, mate!' said Chris. 'You won't jump me so easily a second time.'

'Oh, shuddup, good boy. And keep your voice down. Look, this is getting nowhere. Okay, you could have shopped me but you didn't. You brought me some fodder, and that's fair enough. If I had a medal, I'd pin it on your shirt. Does that satisfy you?'

Chris shrugged sheepishly. 'I only meant I wouldn't help if it meant setting you loose to go on thieving and being a nuisance.'

'I don't go on the nick for fun,' said the boy. 'You've got to live, as the man said. Never mind that. This is something different. All I want is a bit of information.'

Chris hesitated a second. 'Okay,' he said. 'Try me.'

The boy reached for his haversack and delved inside. Out came the rolled socks, the torch, the street map. He flung Chris the map, but didn't explain why, at first. Then he took an envelope from his pocket. He took a shiny rectangle of card from the envelope and handed it over, more carefully.

Chris looked at the picture of a house. He saw the tree in the front – a cherry tree, he thought. He saw the number 17 on the gate and the big man, and the little boy, hand in hand. It took him some moments to recognize the boy.

'You!' he gasped. 'Who's the man?'

'My dad. That was taken six years ago. I was born in that house.'

'So?'

'So I want to find it, and my dad. That's why I bust out of the nick.'

Chris thought this over. 'I don't get it. What's the difficulty, then?'

'I can't remember the address. I was only a kid when I moved, and went to live with these relations in Bristol. That was until I was copped and sent to the School.'

'And your dad still lives there? In that case, why . . .?'

'He had to go away, too. But he came back not long ago.'

54

'How do you know?'

'I had a letter last week. He told me, but he didn't write the address on the letter. He don't know I'm here, of course. You see, he's going abroad, and I want to go with him. He's got married, too. My real mum died when I was a titch, but now I've got a new one. Her name's Audrey. And they're both at the house.'

Chris looked back at the snapshot. It was an ordinary sort of house. There must be hundreds of them around Victoria Station. The boy was going on explaining. 'I got this letter saying they had a chance to go abroad. He didn't say where, exactly, but I reckon it was Australia – somewhere like that. Sheep farming, maybe. My dad always wanted to go to Australia. He thought he couldn't take me yet because of the School. I've another two years to do up there, probably. And I thought to myself, boyo, if you don't move fast you're going to be left behind. They'll be off to the other side of the world, and you'll be stuck over in Bristol playing ping-pong!'

Chris watched the boy as he talked. All his vicious swagger, even his taunting, had disappeared. He was dead serious, anxious, smaller – like the little kid in the photo clutching his dad's hand. Chris said. 'It won't be as easy as that, you know. If you go home, they'll only have to send you back. It would be against the law not to.'

The boy grinned mysteriously. 'My old man'll fix it!'

'But if he took you abroad he'd have to get you a passport – or have your name put on his. There are thousands of formalities.'

'Thousands of what, mate? Oh, well, he'd fix them, too.'

'How?'

'Never mind! I'm not telling you everything, bonzo. Will you help me find my home?'

'It'd take weeks, unless you remember something about the street.'

'I do, mate. It has a sort of foreign name, and I think there's a park on one side. What I want you to do is sing out a few names of streets, and I'll tell you if you come to one I recognize.'

'Haven't you looked yourself?'

'On the map? Yeah, but I'm not much of a reader. I'd only remember the street by the sound of it and I can't pronounce them foreign names.'

'There can't be *that* many,' said Chris. But, when he scanned the street index, there were more than he'd expected; as well as several which the boy, if his reading wasn't too hot, would find hard to get his tongue round.

Chris started near the station, using the square grid, and began reading out the names of streets. He remembered several from his paper round. A few he wasn't sure how to pronounce himself!

The boy shook his head time and again. Sometimes he asked Chris to repeat a street name, but in the end he always rejected it.

'Petit Cochon Street,' said Chris, at last.

'Come again?'

Chris repeated it. 'It's French. It means "Street of the Little Pig".'

'You know French?' The boy looked admiring.

'Not really,' shrugged Chris, bashfully. 'There is a playing field along one side. It belongs to a college.'

The boy looked excited, though not fully convinced. 'Yeah, that rings a bell. I bet that's it!'

'You don't sound too sure.' The boy was running a dirty finger over the map, trying to trace a route from the basement. 'What's the best way of getting there?'

'I wouldn't try it in daylight,' said Chris. 'You'll never make it.'

'Because of the rozzers?' he scoffed, the cockiness returning.

'Don't you believe it, mate. I've been dodging coppers since I was a foot high.'

'It's quiet out there on Sundays,' said Chris. 'You'll stand out like a sore thumb.'

'I'll take my chances.'

'Look, why not let me borrow this photo and go over there? I've got a bike outside. It wouldn't take long. If it *is* Petit Cochon Street I could come back and tell you.'

'And then?'

'Then it's none of my business. You'll be on your own.'

'Yeah . . .' said the boy. 'Yeah, that's fair enough. Ta.'

He seemed doubtful. Chris said. 'You trust me now, don't you? I mean, just to help you find your dad?'

'About as far as I can chuck a skyscraper, mate!'

So much for their cosy little friendship!

'I don't even know your name,' said Chris. 'Mine's Chris.'

'They call me Mousy,' said the boy. Then he grinned again. 'That's on account of me ears!'

He was a rum one all right, decided Chris as he rode away. Mousy? *Foxy*, was more like it! Chris didn't believe half what he'd been told. Either Mousy was lying for some deep purpose of his own, or he had got everything wrong. He couldn't imagine that father and stepmother, if they existed, just welcoming their long lost son with open arms. Of course they'd pack him straight back to that Approved School where he belonged. They couldn't do otherwise.

But in a way that made everything all right – for Chris, he meant. His head had cleared, now. He wasn't aiding a fugitive elude justice. All he was doing was helping Mousy to contact his people. They would do the rest. They would hand Mousy over to the law. The rest was none of Chris's affair.

If the police came into it now, Mousy might be shipped straight back to Bristol without having a chance to see his dad.

To Chris that didn't seem fair. Mousy would have gone through his ordeal for nothing. He had a *right* to see his dad.

As he cycled along the sweltering streets he could see no flaw in this argument, but that didn't stop him feeling vaguely uneasy. He had committed himself to breaking the law, and he was scared – as though he had jumped on a runaway lorry and couldn't find the brake.

He found Petit Cochon Street without much trouble, though this area was Bruce Roper's, not his. Thinking of Bruce made him think of pigeons. Had any of them been rounded up, yet? And what had happened to that albino he'd pursued into the basement? Chris hoped Mousy's straggly old cat hadn't eaten it!

He hadn't really expected to find the house. Yet here it was; a plain, flat semi-detached, facing the playing fields across a deserted width of tarmac: number 17, with a cherry tree at the front. Chris didn't even need to look at the snapshot. So that part of Mousy's yarn was true.

He didn't stop to stare, but rode on past, to the far end of the street; then he doubled back along a parallel road towards the basement hideout.

6 A Miracle, More or Less

Just one hour before Chris Barker found the house in the photo, Beverley Bright had caught Pigeon George, the pied, and was carrying it in the saucepan along the street not far from the Maybe Site. 'Let's see if we can find *another* pigeon,' she'd said, but for the time being one felt enough. The pied seemed to grow fatter and heavier with every step and sometimes Beverley had to plonk the saucepan down on the pavement and give her arms a rest. Her arms always felt shaky and achy afterwards and, as soon as she picked the saucepan up again, it started to wobble.

Still, they got some way towards Monsieur Poirot's lofts and then, suddenly, they heard a strange sound coming from a screen of young poplar trees bordering a small park. Plip-plop, plip-plop, interspersed by laughter and shrill shouts.

'Tennis,' said Beverley.

'Can we watch the tennis, Beverley?' asked Connie.

'You don't know anything about tennis.' But her arms felt as lifeless and droopy as mushroom stalks and the trees looked shady and inviting. 'Well, just for a minute, then.'

It was just a little park with room for two tennis courts

surrounded by an oval-shaped path, and three wooden seats were set on grass verges in front of beds of hydrangeas. Nobody else was watching the tennis. Gladly, Beverley put the saucepan beside one of the seats, and down they sat.

A young man and a young lady were playing on one of the courts. For a little while, Beverley and Connie watched the game. Plip-plop, plip-plop, went the ball. Their heads turned from side to side, the ribbons on their untidy pony tails going to and fro in time with the ball. A long and furious volley was in progress. The young man biffed the ball over the net and the young lady zoomed it back. Their faces were red and intent; they both so badly wanted to win the point.

Suddenly the ball must have caught the edge of the young lady's racquet, because it zoomed up into the air instead of over the net. The young man made some angry remarks. The young lady said it was *his* fault for hitting so hard. Then they both stood there looking up into the sky as though the ball had got stuck up there somewhere and wouldn't come down.

'I know where it went,' said Beverley. 'It went in the flowers.'

'Thanks,' said the young man, seeing them for the first time. He came through the tennis court gate. The young lady followed petulantly. Beverley pointed to the bit of the hydrangea bed she meant, where she had seen the white ball drop. The tennis players poked about with their racquets, but didn't find it. Beverley went along the gravel path to help.

Connie stayed on the seat, sucking her fists. The saucepan of pigeon was beside her, just by the seat, very still. Perhaps Pigeon George was asleep. Perhaps he was dead! Connie stared at the saucepan. Then she squatted down beside the saucepan and put her ear close to the lid. She couldn't hear a sound. Connie got hold of the saucepan handle and gave it a little jiggle. She felt Pigeon George move lumpily about inside, but then he didn't move again. 'Perhaps he's got smuffocated,' thought

Connie. The possibility did not really trouble her. She just wanted to peep and see – see if he *was* smuffocated. Connie didn't like things that ought to move when you jiggled them and didn't.

Very carefully she lifted the tin lid of the saucepan. She moved her nose so that she could peep inside, into that little crescent of darkness and mysterious unmovingness. Then, without warning, with a mad whirl of feathers, Pigeon George burst out of the saucepan, knocking the tin lid clean out of Connie's hand. The lid rolled across the path and spun noisily. Connie stuck her knuckles into her mouth and bawled.

'Oh, Connie!' Beverley heard the lid clatter, saw the feathery fugitive vanish into the poplars. She ran back along the path. The young lady followed, but the young man only glanced up and then went on prodding the hydrangeas with his racquet.

'Is it a *valuable* pigeon?' asked the young lady. Beverley had explained about the saucepan while helping look for the ball. 'You'll be lucky if you get it back, you know. The wild pigeons will get it. That's what happened to our budgie, once. It got out of its cage and the wild birds got it. All we found were a few feathers ...' Connie bawled louder. 'Oh, don't cry! Let's all have a jolly good look. Jim! Did you see where it went?'

'I've got it!' cried the young man, triumphantly trampling down the hydreangeas as he bent forward. Then he waved the lost tennis ball!

'Not the ball – the *bird*, silly!' said the young lady.

Berverley had grabbed the lid, then the saucepan, then Connie, and was running through the gate. They were in the hot street, Beverley running, Connie being dragged. Beverley was sure Pigeon George had got into the street because she had seen him fly for the trees and he wasn't up there now. It was easy to see through the thin branches of the young poplars.

It had been more or less Connie's fault, but Beverley knew

she would get the blame. 'Trust you!' Bruce Roper would say.

They ran on to the corner. Tall, white walls of the deserted buildings glared down. A car hooted. 'Oh, brilliant!' said the hoot. Beverley held the saucepan dangling at her side, the lid tucked under her arm. Connie came grizzling after.

Then Beverley saw Pigeon George. He had come to earth again and was waddling along the pavement. He looked so easy to catch, but the trouble was that just as Beverley got almost within reach, he took off again and flapped fast ahead. He was drawing them far from the tennis park, down in the direction of the Maybe Site. At a corner of the tall fence the pigeon fluttered left, and when Beverley reached the corner he was a whitish dot in the distance, fluttering and waddling past the big bank.

Now Pigeon George was leading them into an area of condemned buildings next to the Maybe Site. The hot sun beat down on shabby walls, broken windows, the jagged shapes of partially demolished houses and offices. Beverley *thought* she saw the pigeon alight on a battered dustbin along one of the alleys, but he wasn't there when they reached the spot.

Instead there was a youth. He had been all alone, leaning against the wall, smoking. The girls' arrival seemed to startle him. He eyed Beverley's saucepan through the smoke, then looked away. He had fair hair and his clothes looked tatty and dusty.

'Please, have you seen a pigeon?' Beverley asked him.

The youth shook his head. He didn't even look at the girls as he did so. He didn't speak. Then he shuffled away along the alley. At the end he stopped, turned round and looked back. He was staring at them, now. As soon as Beverley stared at *him*, though, he glanced away again and sauntered out of sight.

Beverley actually forgot the pigeon. She was wondering. 'I wonder!' she said aloud.

'Wonder what, Beverley?' sniffed Connie.

'I wonder . . .' *Could* it be?

Beverley began moving off along the alley, keeping close to the wall. It *couldn't* be, of course. And yet . . . P.C. Dickie had

told them: 'We don't know much about him. Some say he was only a wee lad, and some say different . . . But we do know he's fair haired . . . !'

And he had chalk on his clothes. *That* chap was fair haired, and his clothes did look chalky. Suppose he was the Pimlico Pilferer!

Beverley got to the top of the alley, and there he was, standing at the far end of another wall, his head turned in their direction. When he saw Beverley staring again he jerked his head away and walked on. This time Beverley ran to the next corner, and sure enough the youth was hurrying ahead, darting those quick, uneasy glances over his shoulder.

'Beverley, come back!' whimpered Connie.

'Sh!' said Beverley. Connie hated to be left behind, even when you were perfectly visible. But now she was afraid Beverley would vanish, for some reason she couldn't understand, and leave her lost and alone in this unfamiliar brick wilderness. Only Beverley knew that they wouldn't get lost. Although it was so different from the streets running near by, they were still close to the Maybe Site. There was even some work going on there, which was unusual. The whine of machinery came across the shattered rooftops, and Big Annie's inquisitive jib swung directly over their heads.

But the area was still a maze, with the alleys and cleared spaces and surviving buildings making no sort of discernible pattern. The youth seemed to know his way about and he was obviously trying to dodge them, now. Beverley had to keep waiting for Connie to catch up, and this would enable the youth to get farther ahead and put more of the twists and turns between them.

He had reckoned without Beverley's doggedness once she had an idea – even a wrong idea – in her head. In any case, she didn't *want* to catch him. What could she do with him if she did? But P.C. Dickie had said, 'I've a hunt on, too.' He thought the Pilferer was hiding somewhere not far away. Why not around here? What better place could there be? If Beverley could discover where exactly he had his hiding place, when he wasn't out on the prowl, then she could soon run and tell the policeman.

So she didn't want to catch him, only keep him in sight. It would be better still if he didn't even know she was behind him any more. And that was what made the chase so comical. The youth knew he was being followed, but he didn't want Beverley to know that he knew. And Beverley didn't want him to know she was following him, was suspicious of him. That meant that whenever, by accident, they happened to face one another along an alley or across a yard, they looked at their feet, or up at the sky, or at an imaginary object in the distance. At least the fugitive didn't stop and angrily challenge her. 'Buzz off!' he *could* have said. 'What are you hounding me for?'

But he didn't, and this made Beverley feel even more sure that she had stumbled on the Pimlico Pilferer himself – and she wasn't going to let him go!

She was beaten in the end, however. The youth reached a broad strip of tangled clearing and suddenly leapt into it and shot across to the far side. Impulsively, Beverley followed, and immediately found herself up to her knees in stinging nettles. The nasty little barbs tore agonizingly into her skin and she dropped the saucepan and stopped – but it was too late to run back. What was worse, Connie had frantically plunged into the nettles behind her, terrified at Beverley's sudden spurt.

Connie screamed; she *hated* nettles, and these were tall, straggly, savage ones. Beverley grasped her under her armpits and lifted her clear, carrying her back to the concrete strip. She bit her lip, knowing that her own legs would soon stop stinging. She had stings only up to her knees, but poor Connie's thighs as well were covered with the huge, white swellings.

She soothed her sister as well as she could, and when the little girl's shrieks had subsided she sat beside her and had a cry herself. That felt better. Then she blew her own nose, and Connie's nose, and remembered that she'd dropped the saucepan and lid in the nettles. She wasn't going in there again to fetch them! But she found a long stick and managed to fish them out. She put the lid on the saucepan, looked at it ruefully, and said mostly to herself, 'No pigeon and no Pilferer!'

After leaving Beverley with Pigeon George, the Chans

crossed St James's Park from Birdcage Walk and headed towards Trafalgar Square. Unlike Pimlico that Sunday morning, the park was full of people. They had practically to push their way through people on the little bridge which crossed the park lake. Jimmy Chan had already bumped several indignant legs with the empty bird cage, and a taxi had almost run Heather Chan over at Admiralty Arch on the Mall.

Trafalgar Square was much safer but even more crowded. It was crowded with tourists and photographers and peanut sellers – and with pigeons, too. But they were all plump, lazy, greedy pigeons – not Monsieur Poirot's sleekly-groomed racers.

The four oval-or-round faces looked seriously around. Heather Chan wanted to feed the pigeons. 'They're overfed already,' grumbled Leo Chan. But he went across and bought some pigeon food. It would have been wrong to give the wild pigeons any of the mixture they had brought for the racers.

When he came back the Chans squeezed on to one of the long seats near the fountains. They fed pigeons. The pigeons waddled up like disreputable little penguins and pecked up the food. Each Chan had a share of the pigeon food. Suddenly a greedier-even-than-most pigeon fluttered up and plopped himself on Heather Chan's shoulder. It landed with such a plop that Heather's arm shook and she dropped her share of the food. Her eyes were filled with tears.

'Don't cry,' said Lena. 'You can have some of mine. Look! The pigeons are coming in *droves*.'

'Now, look carefully all of you,' said Leo Chan. 'Look out for Monsier Poirot's pigeons. White ones, gay pieds, cobbies.'

Pigeon after pigeon – wave on wave – came and pecked up the food Heather had scattered. They worked at it like feathery brooms. They *swept* up the food. The old pigeon who had plopped on Heather's shoulder got none after all. He sat blinking under the seat.

A passing car honked and the whole square broke into a storm of flying pigeons. The bronze lions, even Lord Nelson high on his column, hurriedly put on feather coats. The surface of the big square was suddenly empty of pigeons: there were only crusts and waste paper and droppings – and people, star-

ing up. They stared up to where a few white clouds were being rolled back like sheets. Against the blue coverlet of the sky the pigeons took off and swept back. The Chans looked and looked, but not one of the escaped pigeons could they see.

'Perhaps they wouldn't come here,' said Leo, disheartened. 'Not here, where the wild pigeons would peck them to pieces.'

'They aren't exactly wild, though,' said Lena Chan.

'No,' said Leo. 'But they're like – like a different *race* of pigeons. And hostile – definitely hostile.'

It was after ten o'clock and the great square was thronged; people wearing bright shirts, pretty dresses, colourful, summery hats, and no hats at all. Some were having their photos taken with the pigeons.

The four Chans looked so quaint, thought a young photographer. He had a new camera, an automatic camera. All he had to do was take a photo, count up to ten, and there was the picture to peel off and sell. He wanted to take a picture of the Chans – with pigeons. 'Hey, will you stand all in a line? The tallest on the left, the smallest on the right . . . just be natural. No charge this time. I'll give you the picture free, if you let me take a couple. I want one to put on my advertisement board. Smiles? That's it. Now we'll count ten, and you'll see . . .'

It had all been done so quickly; the smiling row of Chans, the click, the unwinding of the strip of damp film from the reel. The photographer looked at the film himself first. It was a honey! 'How's that?' asked the photographer, proudly.

The Chans looked over his shoulder. There they were, a row of them, with Jimmy holding the bird cage. The pigeons were all around them in the picture. One pigeon was even sitting on Jimmy Chan's shoulder!

Leo Chan saw the pigeon in the picture and darted away. In a second he was wading amongst the pigeons, staring up and down and round and round, even getting down on his knees and peering through people's legs. Had he gone crazy? What had he lost?

'What have you lost?' shouted Lena Chan. Leo didn't hear her. He had almost got *himself* lost, by now – lost in that host of pigeons.

'What's wrong?' demanded the photographer, crestfallen. 'Is there something wrong – with the photo?'

Leo came back. His round face was red. He pointed urgently

at the photo. 'See that pigeon on Jimmy's shoulder – in the picture, I mean? Well, it's an albino, and it's got a ring on it's foot.'

'One of Monsieur Poirot's!' gasped Lena.

'Yeah, and it sat bang on Jimmy's shoulder when the camera clicked. But now it isn't here any more.'

'But it can't be far,' said Lena. They all searched for the albino. It had made that mysterious appearance in the photo, but now its vanishing was just as strange.

'What are you looking for?' asked the photographer.

'A pigeon,' said Lena, absently.

'A *what?*' The photographer was exasperated. Kids, he was thinking. British, American, French, German, Japanese, Chinese . . . he'd met the lot in his time and they were all scatter-brains. There was no fathoming kids. 'Hey, what about the second photo you promised.'

'In a jiff,' called Leo Chan over his shoulder. They were carefully searching the square, entangling themselves in legs, crawling bare-kneed on the hot paving stones of the square.

'Nothing doing,' said Leo, coming back.

'Nothing doing,' agreed Lena.

'What about another picture?' asked the photographer.

'Okay,' said Leo, getting the Chans back in a line.

'Maybe . . .' said Jimmy Chan, his eyes aglint.

'No, it won't happen again!' said Leo, with a sad little laugh. 'That first time was a miracle, more or less.'

It did *not* happen again. This time the camera produced another good picture, but there was no albino pigeon sitting on Jimmy's shoulder. They couldn't expect it.

'Perhaps it flew to the park,' said Leo.

'Or even Buckingham Palace,' laughed Lena. 'We can't look there!'

'Bring the cage, Jimmy,' said Leo. 'Back to the park.'

The photographer said, 'Look, why not leave your cage with

me for a bit? If the pigeon comes back, I'll pop it into the cage and Bob's your uncle.'

'Thanks,' said Leo. 'Jimmy, you stay with the cage. If the gentleman finds the white pigeon, bring it to the park. We'll be waiting by the lake. Okay?'

'Okay,' said Jimmy Chan.

7   After Them!

No Pigeon and no pilferer!

Behind the Maybe Site, the youth had vanished. It was suddenly strangely quiet. Then it wasn't quiet any longer. A new sound came along the alley wall at the end of the clearing – a tinkling, metallic sound accompanied by a faint yelping as a tiny brown puppy, hardly old enough to walk, came limping along the hot strip. There was a tin can tied to its tail, and it was that making the tinkling noises.

The puppy reached them. Beverley grabbed the puppy, quickly slipped the loop of string from its thin little tail and kicked the tin into the nettles. Connie stared, eyes wide. 'Of all the cruel things!' gasped Beverley.

A boy appeared at the end of the alley. 'Hey!' he said, his eyes and mouth stupid. 'You put down that mutt. He's my li'le mutt.' He came stumping towards them, a big, loutish, dark boy with clumsy legs and boots that struck sparks on the concrete.

Beverley thrust the puppy into Connie's arms. Then she picked up the saucepan by its handle and swung it threateningly. 'If you come any nearer I'll whack you with this!'

She called Connie and turned away. They ran along the alley. The boy shouted after them, 'Hey! Where're you going with my li'le mutt?' The scraping boots broke into a clumsy trot.

Connie kept up this time, clutching the shivering puppy to her chest. They turned into the first opening they discovered in the alley wall. They crouched behind the wall. The boy lumbered on past, too stupid to think of looking through the opening. His footsteps died away.

But they didn't hurry out – he might come back. They sat there and Beverley looked round. They were in some sort of a yard. There were piles of tyres and bits of motor cars lying about. The big doors of an old garage building loomed across the yard, and a corrugated iron outbuilding with high windows leaned precariously against a solid brick wall with fragments of broken glass cemented along the top.

Big Annie, the crane's jib, swung back over their heads. The Maybe Site was just across the street on the other side of the garage place. Beverley wondered whether they could find a way through to the other side. If they wanted to avoid that boy, it would be better than using the alleys.

She took Connie round by the side of the garage, along a litter-strewn passageway. But they couldn't get through because there was another wall blocking off the rear of the garage from the street. They retraced their steps back to the yard. And there, one half of the big doors eased open and a face peered out at them. It was a policemen wearing a peaked cap! Perhaps he had heard the sounds outside and was coming to investigate.

'What are you kids doing here?'

He didn't sound too friendly. He didn't look friendly, either. He had a big, square, frowning face. There were sergeant's stripes on the arm of his tunic.

'Oh!' gasped Beverley. 'Are you looking for the Pimlico Pilferer, too?'

Apparently it was a silly question to ask. Beverley realized it as soon as she saw the blank, uncomprehending stare on the sergeant's unfriendly face. It just seemed such a funny place to meet a policeman, and it hadn't occurred to her that he could be there for any different reason.

'What are you talking about?'

Beverley was near the door now. Connie hung back, still clutching the puppy. Beverley saw inside the garage. There was a second policeman, also in a peaked cap. He was standing by a big, blue van. The van had a blue lamp on the top, and that's how she knew it was a police van.

'I just thought . . . you see . . .' Beverley tried to explain, but the words were a jumble. Explaining things was never Beverley's strong point. She always wanted to say so many different things at once. In the end she nearly always had to say them twice.

The sergeant glared at the saucepan, then at Connie. 'Thief?' he said. He half turned. The second policeman's pale face stared out of the gloom. They were both so still, so stiff. The sergeant had strange, hooded eyes that gazed down at Beverley as though she were a creeping thing. 'We don't know nothing about no thief. If it's some game you're playing, scram and play it somewhere else.'

The door slammed. Beverley wondered what she had done wrong. Well, perhaps she had interrupted the policeman doing something important. And they were cross at being interrupted. Whatever it was, it had nothing to do with the Pimlico Pilferer. But they might have understood, been kinder and more patient. They weren't a bit nice, like most policemen, like Dickie Bird, for instance.

'Where are we going now, Beverley?' asked Connie.

'I don't know,' sighed Beverley. 'Away from here for a start.'

'Can we keep the puppy? *Please* let's keep the puppy.'

'We can't. We must take him to the police.'

'Weren't *they* the police?'

'Yes, but I mean the police station. Or P.C. Dickie. The ones in there were different. They had different hats!'

That satisfied Connie. In any case she didn't care about policemen, or pigeons, or even her nettle stings now. All she cared about were puppies. Her whole world was puppies! 'I like him, Beverley. I like stroking him. Oh, he wriggles, and tickles!'

They put him in the saucepan and he curled up at once and fell asleep, panting in the heat of the yard.

'Shall we put the lid on, Beverley?'

'Yes, he can breathe through the holes in the bottom. But I'll carry him.'

This time Beverley held the saucepan beneath her arm. The puppy was heavier than Pigeon George. They found their way out of the maze of alleys. Connie ran beside Beverley, every now and then lifting the saucepan lid to see if the puppy was awake. In the end Beverley slapped her hand. 'Stop fussing with him!'

She was fed up. She felt useless and silly because she had had a lot of useless and silly adventures and nothing to show for them except stinging legs and a puppy that would have to be given to the police.

Beyond the Maybe Site she started looking for Dickie Bird. She was still sure it had been the Pimlico Pilferer she'd chased, and if those other policemen weren't interested, P.C. Dickie would be.

As they hurried along towards Victoria Street Big Ben struck eleven.

Only *three* Chans had actually reached the Park. When they got to the lake they flung themselves on the grass near the water. Not far away across the water was a small neck of land, which people called the island – though it wasn't quite. But you had to walk some way round the bank to the spot where you could reach it on foot. The three Chans were separated from the neck by several yards of water – and it looked pretty deep. Several little islets of piled stones were dotted between them and the bigger island.

On the island were some pelicans with snowy-pink, untidy feathers. The surface of the water sometimes broke, like stones breaking windows, as fish in the depths swallowed specks of food. An echelon of ducklings set out for the island under the willows, swimming far from the iron-and-stone bridge with its feet in the water – the bridge leading to Pimlico. A large duck came skimming after them. The ducks sped, leaving wide 'Vs' of wake behind them, and ripples hurried to extinction against the banks. But one duckling stayed behind, cleaning its feathers, and there it floated, all alone, like a solitary sailor in a dinghy. More and more people were arriving, carrying lunch baskets, bundles and cameras. The deck chairs on the grass were soon all used up.

Leo Chan said, 'If I was one of Monsieur Poirot's pigeons, you wouldn't catch me coming here. Look at the people. Hark at the noise!'

Only Heather Chan, the smallest, was actually looking for pigeons. She was thinking of her brother Jimmy and the wonderful way he had found a pigeon while being photographed in Trafalgar Square. Perhaps the pigeons had flown away into some magical, *other* world – a world as magic as cameras. While pigeons were in *that* world, they couldn't be in *this* one, could they? They couldn't be sitting in ordinary trees or waddling across ordinary grass.

Now Heather had her eye on a very young lady wearing a polka-dot miniskirt. She was taking snapshots of the ducks on the lake. She was very pretty and she had sparks in her eyes.

Heather left the other Chans and crept closer. Now she was

very close to the polka-dot girl and the polka-dot girl was right on the edge of the bank, aiming her camera at the island, digging in her heels, bracing herself on the edge.

Then Heather saw the pigeon! It was coming towards them along the bank. She saw the ring glinting on its foot, and Bruce Roper had said, 'Look for pigeons with rings on their feet' and Leo Chan had said the same, so Heather had heard it twice and there could be no mistake. *This* pigeon had a ring on its foot!

'Oh!' said Heather, then she slipped. Her front foot was much too close to the edge of the water; it slipped on the slippery edge which was wet with the coming and going of ducks and pelicans. In she went – into the lake!

'Oh, my!' cried the polka-dot girl. Leo and Lena turned, saw what had happened and raced to the edge. Heather was standing up to her tummy in water. She wasn't crying, only shivering. Her oval eyes were wide and startled.

Leo went straight in. He didn't even bother to take off his socks and shoes. But he couldn't reach Heather because she was walking on, through the deepening water, towards one of the little stone islets. The pigeon had taken off and flown to the islet.

'Turn round – come back!' yelled Leo. 'Lena, grab my hand. Oh, you'll have to come in, too!'

'All right,' nodded Lena. She turned to the polka-dot girl. 'Please will you hold my hand?'

'Oh, yes!' said the polka-dot girl. Lena got into the water. She didn't remove her shoes and socks, either. She grasped Leo's hand. The polka-dot girl was holding *her* hand. Now they made a human chain out into the lake, but even then Leo only just managed to reach Heather. Heather was wading on and on towards the stone islet. She was pointing with a dripping, shivering, stumpy finger. 'Pigeon . . . there!' she said.

Then Leo saw the cobbie. His eyes grew bigger. Carefully he drew Heather back until he was able to link her fingers in

Lena's. Now he let go – he was on his own. Leo was not far from the islet.

'Leo!' cried Lena. She had known what Leo planned to do and she was afraid – a little. The stone islet was not far, but who knew how deep the water was out there?

But it wasn't very deep. Almost at once, Leo reached the islet, reached across and seized the cobbie and gathered it in his wet grasp.

Then he called back, 'It's Pigeon David, the cobbie. Where's Jimmy? Lena, go and find Jimmy. We want the cage.'

When the others had left, Jimmy sat under one of the bronze lions, parking the old bird cage between his feet. He even left the side open and it wasn't long before some old, grey, careworn inhabitant of the square came up and waddled right inside. Jimmy picked up the cage and shook him out.

'You aren't allowed to take those pigeons home, sonny,' said an elderly, fussy gentleman. He carried a notebook. He wore a tweedy hat, and tiny steel-rimmed spectacles perched on his nose. He sat down next to Jimmy and gave him a little Nature lesson. Jimmy hardly understood a word of it but he was too shy and too frightened to get up and go in the middle of it.

'These pigeons are mostly *feral* pigeons. They're descended from rock doves. That's why they feel so much at home among all these tall buildings. The buildings, to them, are rather like cliffs, you see. Tall stone cliffs with window ledges for perches . . . you won't take one of these pigeons home, will you?'

Jimmy nodded his promise. The elderly gentleman gave him a mint-with-a-hole, then shuffled off, writing in his notebook. Jimmy sucked. Soon he got fed up. He couldn't see over the heads of the people even from the lion's plinth. A lot of *them* were on the plinth, too. The lion looked disagreeable and disapproving. Jimmy had had enough.

The Day of the Pigeons

He grabbed the cage by its ring and carried it off in the direction of the Mall. The Mall was the quickest way to St James's Park, but Jimmy got pushed and jostled by the crowds making for the zebra crossings leading to Whitehall. And it was hopeless trying to find his way out of that milling throng, without *really* trying. Jimmy did not feel like trying. He just drifted with the tide of chattering sightseers; the side of the bird cage had come out of its slots and he was half crouched among the legs, trying to make running repairs.

The crowd thinned out a little and here was Jimmy along Whitehall. And there, unbelievably, only a few yards ahead was a ringed pigeon! It was one of the albinos – surely the same one which posed for the photograph on Jimmy's shoulder. (It was Pigeon Oswald, who had had enough of the crowded Square.)

Jimmy went after it, zig-zagging through the people, not daring to take his eyes off the pigeon in case it somehow magically vanished. Suddenly it stopped, cocked its head on one side, and waddled slowly across the pavement and disappeared from view – but not for long. Jimmy caught up and saw the pigeon had gone into one of the stone arches which stood at the entrance to Horse Guards. It was the arch where the mounted Life-Guard was on duty.

Jimmy looked up at the splendid figure on the sleekly groomed chestnut horse. The Life-Guard wore a silver helmet with a white plume, and over his red tunic gleamed a plated-steel breast-plate. He had long, black, shiny jack-boots and white breeches. He sat very still on his saddle, a gleaming sword in his hand, the naked blade resting on his right shoulder. Several sightseers were taking snapshots but the Life-Guard took no notice – he was used to it.

The horse took no notice, either. The big eyes rolled slowly and watchfully behind the blinkers, but that was all. The eyes seemed to be watching Jimmy Chan. Jimmy looked away –

then he saw the pigeon. Pigeon Oswald was pecking at the bits of straw on the pavement just outside the sentry's arch. There was plenty of room, plenty of bits, if only Pigeon Oswald hadn't been so inquisitive! Now he waddled right up to one of the horse's hoofs and pecked at that!

The horse soon grew annoyed and began chomping up and down with his front hoofs. The Life-Guard swayed and joggled a little, but still kept his eyes front. Pigeon Oswald nearly got stamped on by those angry, chomping hoofs, but he was far too stupid to notice. There was his silly, bird-brained head jerking up and down, up and down, like the head of a cardboard cut-out bird. Several of the sightseers saw and laughed, and the Life-Guard's face turned a faint pink behind his chin strap.

Jimmy put the cage by the arch. He knew he had to catch the pigeon before it got squashed flat by those angry, chomping hoofs. He stooped, crept forwards near the arch – so close to the horse's flank that he could feel the steamy sweat on his face. He tried to grab the pigeon. He nearly got his hand stamped on by the horse. The horse began to rear. The pink, silent Life-Guard clutched the reins and even his sword wobbled. But Jimmy got the pigeon – got it tight in his hands before backing away across the pavement. The voice seemed to come from nowhere; the Life-Guard certainly didn't move his lips. But he glared down at Jimmy, and the mysterious voice said, ' 'Op it, quick, or I'll 'ave you locked up in the Tower of London!'

8 The Man at the Maybe Site

The sun was getting high when Chris reached Mousy's hideout. As he crawled through the basement a hot, unsavoury stench rose from the bundles of rags, and when he gained the broken door into the garden the sun struck his face like a gun flash.

The cat dozed on the wall. Mousy was waiting, watching. He said nothing, but his eyes were questioning.

'Yeah,' said Chris. 'It's the right street. I found your house.'

Mousy breathed, nodded. Then he gave Chris an oddly suspicious glance, opened his map and ran his finger over it. He found the marked street all right. He seemed to be calculating the distance. In the silence Chris could hear the insects in the long grass making sounds like violin strings.

Then Mousy refolded the map and said, 'Ta, mate, Ta very much. You can hop it, now, if you want to. I can manage.'

Chris didn't move. He was thinking what a filthy state the boy was in. The heat had made everything worse. Sweat had tangled his hair, turning the dirt on his face into mud. Ants were crawling about on his clothes having a banquet on the specks of flour Mousy hadn't managed to brush off.

'You can't go out – like that,' said Chris.

Mousy knew what he meant. He grinned wryly. 'Just show me the way to the bathroom, mate!'

Chris said, 'Look, there's just one more thing I don't mind doing. I could call at the house and give your people a message. It isn't likely they'll both be out on Sunday morning, is it?'

'How should I know?' Mousy scratched his neck, thinking. The grimy face changed expression several times. 'What would you tell them, exactly?'

'Anything you like. Your dad could come here and pick you up maybe. Has he got a car?'

For some reason Mousy smirked. 'I told you, bonzo. I don't know anything about things like that. But I expect so.'

'What's their name? I mean who do I ask for?'

'Lawson.' He revealed his surname grudgingly.

'What sort of work does your dad do?'

Again the exasperating grin. 'You mean now? When I was a titch he used to work on buildings. He was in a demolition squad. When I wasn't at school he used to cart me around with him a lot, and that's how I remember. He doesn't do that now, though – work on building sites, I mean. And he's got a new job . . .'

'Yes, you told me,' said Chris. 'Sheep farming in Australia, wasn't it?'

'Well, that was a sort of guess,' admitted Mousy. Then he added, as though it was important that Chris knew, 'He's smart, is my dad. Nobody don't push *him* around.'

'Well, I'll be off, then,' said Chris.

'Watch it, boyo. Don't go at it like a bull in a china shop. If my folks aren't at home, don't do anything, see?'

'Oh, shuddup!' said Chris. Mousy wasn't going to push *him* around, either.

Chris picked up his bicycle at the corner. A new worry nagged at his mind on the way to Petit Cochon Street. Suppose

Mousy's people were the sort who wanted to pamper him, regardless? Suppose they hid him in the attic, trying to shield him from the authorities, telling the police he wasn't there? He, Chris Barker, would be in a spot if anyone found out he'd helped a fugitive – and they probably would find out.

He didn't see Angus this trip. He avoided the busier streets. Far off to his left he saw Big Annie's gigantic jib sniffing the

rooftops like an inquisitive dinosaur. 'The Street of the Little Pig' was deserted, the long row of semi-detached houses staring boredly across at the empty playing field. He rode past Number 17 several times before finding the courage to walk through the gate.

The cherry tree had a few cherries on it, but the birds had

83

got most of them. The gate had to be shoved hard before it opened. He pressed a bell-push at the door side and heard it ring.

The door opened about six inches and a woman peered out through heavily mascaraed eyes. She had a hard face, lots of make-up, lacquered finger nails and piles of false hair. Chris reckoned she was nothing like so young as she wanted to be.

'What do you want?'

'Is Mr Lawson in?'

'No . . . who wants to know?'

'I've got a message – from Keith.'

'Keith?' The name obviously meant nothing at first. Then the woman's eyes widened. 'Keith! Oh my . . .' She opened the door wider, looking quickly to and fro along the empty street. Her gaze came back to Chris, anxious, or suspicious. 'You mean Keith Lawson? But he's away at – at school.'

Chris grinned awkwardly. 'Yeah, but he got out . . .'

'And you too?'

'Oh, no – I just happened to come across him. He's hiding. He wants to come home, but . . . well, I said I'd make sure it was all right. You see, we weren't sure this was the right house.'

This was the house all right. This was Mousy's stepmother, and he was welcome! She was looking at Chris as though he had just crawled from under a stone. She had on a fancy red dress with an imitation diamond brooch – all very smart for a hot Sunday morning. Was she ready to go somewhere? Chris could see a large travelling case sitting by the staircase.

'We don't want nothing to do with Keith,' she said. 'He's trouble! Whoever you are, you go back to him and tell him to hop it back to Bristol, not to show his face here.'

Chris said, 'It's really Mr Lawson I wanted to see.'

'I told you, he isn't here, and he won't be.'

'Oh? Well, perhaps I could go and see him . . .'

'No, you can't. Getting a bit cheeky, aren't you? I told you what you had to do . . . where did you say Keith was?'

'I didn't say,' said Chris, and made for the gate. The door shut hard behind him, but the whiff of cheap perfume still lingered.

For some moments he sat on his bike, gripping stickily at the handlebar grips. His knees felt wobbly. He'd made a mess of things, somehow. What was he going to tell Mousy – about the home he had wanted, about his stepmother? That tarted-up woman didn't want Mousy and Chris was no nearer locating Lawson.

He suddenly sensed a movement at the window. The curtains had shuddered and Mousy's stepmother was peeping out. She had put on a hat. Chris got it! She wanted to come out, go somewhere in a hurry, but she didn't want to start till Chris had gone.

Chris obliged. Pretending he hadn't noticed her at the window he rode away casually, stopped just around the corner, parked his bicycle and returned to view the stretch of the road. He was just in time to see Mrs Lawson emerge from the gate, give a quick glance behind her in his direction, then step out fast along the pavement.

Where was she going? To find Lawson? It seemed a good bet, unless . . . unless she was going to the police about Mousy. No – if she'd had that idea she'd have telephoned. Chris noticed the wire sagging down from insulators over the upstairs windows.

Chris waited till she had turned the far corner of the street, then he ran for his bike and followed. Of course, the woman might catch a taxi, or a bus – it depended where she was going. But she hadn't brought the suitcase, so it was unlikely that this journey was the one she had dressed up for. She was making it because of Chris's call – because of Keith Lawson!

It was a long walk, but an easy bike ride. She seemed too

occupied with her thoughts to look round again, and all Chris had to do was pedal gently along to keep her in view. Across Victoria Street, turning right then up towards the Maybe Site.

She stopped at the Maybe Site! Chris hadn't thought of that. But if she was after Lawson then something Mousy had said clicked into place. 'When I was a titch he used to work on buildings.' But that had been six years ago or more. Mousy thought his father had given that work up. Was he wrong?

Chris braked sharply, pulled in near the corner of the fence and watched. Mrs Lawson was rapping on the big gate. Was it

locked, then? It was odd, thought Chris, to keep the site gate locked when work was going on inside. Big Annie, the crane, was busy unloading a huge truck parked farther along the fence.

The gate opened, let the woman through, then closed behind

her. Chris jumped, grasped the top of the fence and heaved himself up. Now he could see across the site to the timber office building. Coming towards it was Mousy's stepmother accompanied by a big, bulky man with brown arms thrust out of a red chequered shirt.

The man in the photo . . . Lawson, Mousy's dad? Yes, he was some distance away but Chris was pretty sure that's who it was. So if he wanted to meet Mousy's father and tell him where his son was, he would have to get into the Maybe Site. But not yet – not while his unwelcoming stepmother was there.

Beverley and Connie found Angus, but he was difficult to talk to. He was trying to tell a long crocodile of foreign visitors that the best way to Buckingham Palace was *not* across Vauxhall Bridge. What with their Scandinavian tongues and Angus's Scots accent, communication was uneasy.

'What's that?' he asked, during a short intermission before a second wave of lost pilgrims descended upon him. '*What puppy?*'

Beverley obligingly removed the saucepan lid as though inviting Angus to taste the stew. Then she went into a long and involved explanation, as only Beverley could.

'Do you mind saying all that again?' asked Angus. Beverley made a fresh start. The policeman half looked at the puppy curled up contentedly in the saucepan. 'Weel, you keep him for the time being. I'll let you know if we get a lost-dog report. As he's such a wee creature I don't suppose there's a licence . . . you found him *weer?*'

'Near a garage place, not far from the Maybe Site. That's where we followed the Pimlico Pilferer, we think. I mean, we think it was the thief. But the police sergeant said . . .'

'What police sergeant?'

'The one in the garage, with the police van. It had a light on top. He wasn't a bit interested in the Pimlico Pilferer . . .'

'You chased the thief?' Angus was getting quite interested. 'And he tied a tin to the puppy's tail?'

'No!' giggled Beverley. 'That was a different boy.'

Then the third wave of visitors arrived and Angus was swept away.

'Did you hear?' said Beverley. 'We can keep the puppy – for a little while, anyway.'

Connie's eyes sparkled. 'What shall we call him, Beverley?'

'I don't care. You think of a name as we go along.'

'Can we call him Noddy?'

'All right, then – Noddy. But he'll hate you for it when he grows as big as a horse!'

Near the Maybe Site they ran into Chris, who had just climbed down after catching that glimpse of the Lawsons. Beverley rattled out much the same tale as she'd told Angus. She showed him the puppy, too, but Chris only nodded. From what she said, Chris was quite sure the youth she had chased was no more Mousy than he was. But he didn't tell her so.

'You told Dickie Bird all that? You absolute twerp!'

Beverley looked hurt. 'What did I do wrong?'

'Oh, never mind.' Chris was wondering about those other policemen with the van. Beverley could hardly have made all *that* up. Could they be on the look out for Mousy? It was possible. On the other hand, they were staying under cover near the Maybe Site; they were nowhere near the basement.

Of course, with the van they could get anywhere they wanted, if they received information about the fugitive's whereabouts, especially on Sunday with the streets down there practically clear of traffic. Perhaps they *had* some information by now. Chris knew that after an escape the police stations were circularized and asked to keep a look out for a fugitive. Had Dickie Bird seen a circular yet?

But why were those coppers hiding in a garage?

Beverley asked, 'Do you think we should go on looking for the Pimlico Pilferer? Isn't he more important than pigeons?'

'I wouldn't,' said Chris, keeping a straight face. The quicker Beverley's interest in Mousy was killed the better. 'I've heard that he carries a knife, and if you get too close he chucks pepper in your eyes. You stick to pigeons!'

When the girls had gone out of sight, Chris pedalled slowly towards the basement. He had better warn Mousy about that van. And what was he going to tell him about his precious Aunt Audrey?

The woman had gone straight off to see Lawson, presumably to tell him that that Keith was in town. What did that mean? Was Lawson going to be pleased – or not? Why hadn't she wanted Chris to know where Lawson was? But now Chris did know, and as soon as he could he would have to contact Mousy's father and hear what he had to say.

It would be better to tell Mousy nothing until Chris had seen Lawson. There were things he had to find out. Meanwhile, why had 'Aunt Audrey' behaved so cagily? Was it merely that she was jealous of Keith Lawson and didn't want him home, to come between her and her new husband? In that case, who could tell what she had told Lawson!

It was all a puzzle. Chris felt annoyed again – annoyed with himself and a bit scared. Mousy Lawson was a crook. It was no use thinking of his hunted face and feeling sorry for him. Chris should have done the only sensible thing – handed him over to the law. It wasn't as though that Approved School was a prison, was it? It was a place where kids like Mousy got straightened out. Chris wasn't sure that the idea always worked – that kids like Mousy were automatically turned into angels overnight. But at least they had a chance to learn, there; learn to stop thieving and busting things and being tearaways.

So helping Mousy was breaking the law and whatever Chris's excuses it was wrong. Chris told himself this over and over; yet he had the feeling that there was another truth, perhaps more important, though he didn't quite reach what it was. When he tried to think it out, all he could see was Mousy Lawson's cocky face, which so often changed to fright, hurt and longing.

The old cat was sitting at the top of the basement steps. It gave Chris a vague look of reproach. Below, in the garden, Mousy was squatting on the box scowling at the open map. He scarcely glanced up at Chris, though he must have checked it was him coming through the basement.

Chris lied at once. 'There was nobody in; I'll try again later.'

'Suit yourself, mate.'

The filthy hands made fists on the map, which was getting screwed up and torn. What had happened to the boy's half-friendliness, the beginning of trust? What was he brooding about now?

Chris said, 'Well, I did my best, didn't I?'

'Sure, sure!'

'Look, Mousy. You've got to face it. When I get you to your mum and dad, they may make you go back.'

'Yeah?' Mousy glowered. 'They'd better not do that, bonzo. Anyway, my old man won't shop me.' And he grinned again. Why?

Chris hesitated over the next bit. 'Suppose he did ... send you back. Well, that school isn't really a nick, is it? I mean, they were trying to help you.'

'Do me a favour!' drawled Mousy. 'You talk like my probation officer that was. You won't believe it but her name was Gertrude, and she had whiskers.' The expression changed again. 'I'm not saying she was a bad old pumpkin, but she couldn't half preach.'

'*I'm* not preaching.'

'Shuddup, then.'

There was the background drone of traffic in Victoria Street. The insects in the garden buzzed discordantly. Above them a window shot open startlingly and the head of a mop appeared, was shaken briefly, then withdrawn. A shower of dust and feathers settled on them. They both laughed and Mousy, his mood over, leaned back against the wall, his bloodshot eyes now fixed on the intense blue sky.

He said, 'We had a rough old garden a bit like this over in Bristol, where I lived with them relations. I went there when I was seven. I don't remember my mum, much. She died when I was three. My dad had to go away, so they pushed me off to Bristol. Those relations weren't bad, but you see, there were these two kids, a snotty-nosed pair who had it in for me. All the years we were together, we never got on, like. The boy was a creep. Douglas his name was, and he was always picking on me, getting me in trouble with his old man. One day I thumped him – I didn't half thump him! Well, my uncle – that's what I called him, anyway – gave me a belting because I made the kid's nose bleed, though he was bigger than me. So I skipped.'

'How old were you then?'

'Nearly twelve. It's a wonder I stuck it so long. Anyway, I never went back. They called the cops out, of course. They practically got the fire brigade, but I managed to stay loose for weeks, playing truant from school and all. I got up a gang. We were real terrors. Boy! we near enough ran that town. Then some kids shopped us and I was sent to the School. That was over a year ago.'

'What I don't get,' said Chris, 'is what your dad was doing all that time. Didn't he come and see you?'

'He couldn't,' said Mousy, unusually diffident. 'But we wrote letters sometimes. He was – away.'

'Where, abroad?'

'Well, sort of. The Isle of Wight.'

Even then Chris didn't get it. 'What was he doing there?'

'Stitching mailbags, I suppose. He was in clink, you dope! Didn't you guess?'

'No . . .' Yet it all seemed so obvious now. 'But about this job in Australia . . .'

'Or somewhere,' Mousy corrected him. 'Well, I reckon he's going straight, now. I mean, now he's got married and all that. He's come back to our old house, just for a while before he fixes this new job. I told you.'

'Yeah, you did,' said Chris, and got up.

Mousy looked alarmed. 'Where to now?'

'I'll try the house again.' But really he just wanted to get away and think.

Mousy said, 'When you come back, reckon you could bring some water, and a lump of soap? I should have nicked some yesterday while I had the chance.'

'See what I can do,' said Chris. 'Don't go away!'

So Mousy wanted to wash his filthy face before meeting his dad; the dad who had been a gaol bird. No wonder Mousy had been so sure Lawson wouldn't send him back to Bristol. An ex-convict wouldn't want to help the police.

Or did it make any difference? If Lawson had served his sentence, and was now planning to lead a normal life in a new country, maybe Mousy was in for a nasty surprise. Lawson might not want to attract fresh trouble by harbouring a fugitive son.

It all depended – on things Chris still didn't know. He cycled towards his home, wondering what to do next. He couldn't help feeling that whatever he did he was getting drawn deeper and deeper into something dangerous – something he couldn't control.

He'd have to see Lawson, find out how the man felt, what he was planning to do with Mousy now he knew he was in London and on the run. But Chris decided to 'stall' for a bit longer.

He'd fetch Mousy his soap and water, first. Then he'd ask Mousy why his father had been to prison; he should have asked before. It would help, when he met Lawson, to know what kind of man he was.

9 Pigeons Underground

Eventually Beverley and Connie arrived at Monsieur Poirot's lofts.

'We haven't any pigeons,' said Beverley to Bruce. 'But you should hear what's happened . . .'

Bruce heard, but he wasn't really interested in thieves, only pigeons. 'I'm glad you've turned up. Here's the bean pole. *You* can keep the cats away for a bit. Sid and I are going after pigeons.'

'Do you want to borrow my saucepan?'

'No thanks. Have you seen the Chans lately?'

'No, but we met Chris. Chris is funny peculiar all of a sudden, as if he's up to something. He was down at the Maybe Site. I wonder why?'

'Looking for pigeons, I hope!' said Bruce. 'Well, cheerio. Look out for that tabby from next door. Give it a good poke if it comes over.'

'Can we put the puppy in one of those empty nest boxes?'

'Help yourself. Come on, Sid. Let's go.'

Sidney had had his face washed twice and his hair combed once. His fringe made him look quite angelic. The Ropers' mother had given them milk and biscuits – to keep-you-going-and-don't-be-late-for-dinner, she said – but dinner was always late on Sundays.

Bruce left his bike behind because he wasn't supposed to let Sidney ride on the crossbar except in back streets. And if they were going after pigeons, who knew what sort of streets they would have to go along? Besides, they had one of Monsieur Poirot's travelling baskets and that was far too big to be tied on a bike. They had to carry it by its handles, one at each end. On one side, in large, red letters, was stapled a strip of card:

LIVESTOCK – TO BE CALLED FOR

On the rare occasions that Monsieur Poirot actually entered pigeons in a race, he sent them by train to the starting point and they travelled in this basket. The basket was light enough and they had no trouble carrying it, except that at Sidney's end it kept bumping on the pavement because he was so short.

More logical and pigeon-conscious than anybody else, Bruce took a spiralling route out from the lofts, covering every accessible street, garden, yard and space. Sidney padded loyally along with his end of the basket, but even Bruce had to admit, after nearly an hour of this, that it was a waste of effort. They saw no pigeons. They didn't even see Chris, or the Chans. Bruce was beginning to have a nasty vision of kind, blustery, portly Monsieur Poirot returning from the continent. Monsieur Poirot hated wringing pigeons' necks, maybe; but he would positively enjoy wringing Bruce's.

Eventually Bruce grew tired of going round more or less in circles so he broke off at a tangent and headed in the St James's Park direction. It was in Petty France that he saw the pigeon; Pigeon Henry, the chequered. He had come floating down from a rooftop, rather like a slightly damaged parachute. He landed awkwardly on the pavement, righted himself, then jiggled and joggled along in a quaint series of dots and carries.

Bruce plodded eagerly after him, dragging Sidney and the basket behind him. Pigeon Henry heard them coming, took a sudden turn and fluttered into the street under the wheels of a passing taxi.

'Oh, brilliant!' gasped Bruce. All he could see were feathers – feathers everywhere.

'He's got runned over, Brucie,' announced Sidney.

'No he hasn't,' cried Bruce, pointing. 'There he goes. Oh, crumbs!' Pigeon Henry had vanished through the entrance to the underground station. Bruce and Sidney dashed in after it and were just in time to see him making for the flight of steps leading down to the platforms.

Several illuminated ticket machines stood in a row, like polite daleks waiting to be fed. Bruce ignored them. There wasn't time to worry about unimportant things like tickets. Basket and all, they raced past the unoccupied ticket barrier and down the steps. But by that time Pigeon Henry was nowhere to be seen. They were on the 'up' platform. They put the basket down and stared in both directions.

At the far end the platform continued into a dark, cavernous extension. Along there it was aglow with signal lamps and dusty bulbs. Between the boys and this far end was a porter with a bucket and a long-handled brush. He had started from the cavern end of the platform and was working his way along, repainting the white edge of the platform.

It was uncannily silent. The long brush swished faintly. A few well-behaved travellers stood waiting for the next train; workmen on the Sunday shift, a group of foreign sightseers, a tall, sad-faced bearded man with a walking stick who was watching the porter paint.

Bruce held Sidney's hand and they searched the platform half-way along and back, listening for the slightest sound of

rustling wings or coo-ings. Then a red-faced man and his wife and three squeaking children tore down the stairs, and that was the end of listening.

'He ain't down here, Brucie,' said Sidney, at the top of his voice.

The porter heard him, looked up and asked, 'Who are you looking for, then?' He eyed the basket uneasily.

'A pigeon,' said Bruce. 'We followed it into the station.'

The porter stuck his brush into the bucket of white paint and put his hands on his hips. 'There aren't any pigeons down here, so beat it!'

'There it goes!' said the bearded man, pointing with his stick. 'There! Under the rails.'

Everybody looked down at the rails. Pigeon Henry was waddling along in the cement trough between the rails. A live electric rail gleamed only inches above its jerking head.

'Stand well back, there,' said the porter, because everybody was leaning over the platform edge looking at Pigeon Henry. 'And don't step on my new painted strip, if you don't mind.'

'Can't you get it out?' inquired the bearded man.

'It'll be electrocuted!' cried the woman.

The porter grinned. 'Not unless it puts one foot on the live rail, and his other foot on one of them *other* rails!' he pointed out. That was a joke, because the rails were so far apart.

'What about when a train comes?' said the woman.

'It'll be electrocooted, yes?' asked a foreign gentleman.

'Electrocooted, no,' said the porter. 'Not unless . . .'

A throbbing roar came from the dark cavern beyond the lights. A train burst out, thrusting its ugly head into the station. Nobody could bear to look at Pigeon Henry down in the trough.

The doors hissed open. Nobody got off, and nobody got on, either. They all dreaded what might have happened to Pigeon Henry, but nobody was going to miss finding out.

The doors hissed shut. The train roared on. 'He's all right!' cried the woman. 'There he goes. He'll be in the tunnel in a minute.'

'Now then, stand back!' said the porter.

Bruce said, 'Please go and get him for us.'

'I'm not going down there,' grunted the porter, reaching for his brush. 'Not after a blooming pigeon, I'm not. They'd have to switch off the current, and they won't do that. Not for a blooming pigeon. He'll be all right, if he keeps his head down.'

'Monstrous!' observed the bearded man.

One of the workmen said, 'Why not stick your broom down there? Maybe the pigeon'll hop on board. Then you can pull him out.'

'Oh, sure, and I get a big enough shot of electricity up my arm to light up Picadilly Circus!'

'Ridiculous,' said the bearded man. 'The broom's wood, and wood isn't a conductor of electricity. I'll go down and get the pigeon.'

'No you won't,' said the porter. 'The public's not allowed on them rails.'

'Here comes another train,' said a workman.

The fat man's children started to cry. 'Shuddup squeaking,' said the fat man. 'You're always squeaking. We're getting on this train, pigeon or no blessed pigeon.'

The train arrived. Nobody could bear to look except Bruce. He *made* himself look. He saw Pigeon Henry suddenly take to his wings and fly out of the trough. His wings must have brushed against the thrusting buffers of the second train. But he was out of the trough. The wind from the rushing train bowled him over like a bundle of feathers. Then he staggered upright and waddled away towards the cavernous extension of the platform.

'Come on Sid – leave the basket,' yelled Bruce. Away they

ran, after Pigeon Henry, following him into that strange cavern of will-o'-wisp lights.

They kept him in view for several seconds, while the bustle went on behind them on the platform. Nobody noticed Bruce and Sidney as they groped on and on into the dimness.

They passed several steel doors which were marked with mysterious numbers and code letters and it was right at the end, before the extension finally dissolved into the pitch darkness of the tunnel mouth, that they discovered one door which had been left slightly ajar.

Either Pigeon Henry had fluttered off into the tunnel, from which the train had just emerged, or he had crept through this door – he definitely wasn't on the rails. Bruce pushed open the door and in they went. They were in a narrow corridor lined with panels of switches and dials that might easily have belonged to a time machine, or the more advanced type of earth satellite.

'Did he come in 'ere, Brucie?' yelled Sidney. Sidney would shout in a cathedral.

'Hush, Sid,' said Bruce. 'I think so. Let's go along and see.'

At the end of the corridor were stone stairs leading down. At the bottom the boys could turn either left or right at a dimly lit T junction, and Bruce chose left. He thought he could hear Pigeon Henry along there but he was far from sure.

A few yards along the light practically gave out altogether. Bruce saw the whale's mouth of some kind of enormous pipe ahead.

'Come on, Sid,' he said. His voice came back at him, whirled into senseless syllables by the echoing metal tube. He got down on his knees and crawled, feeling smooth-headed rivets under his hands. A stream of pungent air whistled along the pipe, howling softly in his ears. He sensed Sidney crawling more noisily behind him. It seemed a long time before they got to the end of this pipe. Bruce swung his plump body round on its seat, and groped cautiously with his legs to find what sort of foothold offered itself beyond.

A greenish, phosphorescent light from an air vent revealed a brick-lined tunnel. Some kind of fungus grew on the walls, and here and there tufts of rotten wires seemed to sprout out of the brickwork. Bruce had a guess at what sort of place they were in: some ancient and long-abandoned service gallery belonging to the old underground railway, maybe.

He forgot all about Pigeon Henry. Something else held his attention. Sounds . . . sounds far ahead along the gallery. They were confused because of the odd effect of their echoes. There were tappings, but the tappings echoed several times so that they came back with staccato frequency from all directions at once.

And voices.

'Who's that, Brucie?' asked Sidney.

'Some men working down here, I suppose, Sid. Be quiet!' The whispers of his own voice eddied around them.

Then the tappings were repeated, followed by more of the alien, distorted voices: 'Tis scrabbly-abbly-abbly . . .'

'Cobblestones-stones-stones-stones . . .'

'Cornflakes an' kippers-ippers-ippers . . .'

Bruce grabbed Sidney and together they started backing away along the tunnel. On and on, stern first, heads bent, until eventually it dawned on Bruce that they had missed the mouth of the pipe. Worse! In Bruce's anxiety to follow the course of the gallery wall, they seemed to have turned an extra corner somewhere.

And soon they were hopelessly lost.

10 The Streets have Eyes

It was some time after his exchanges with the foreign visitors and his encounter with Beverley Bright that Angus had the opportunity to sift through what he had been told. Perhaps that scatterbrained girl really had caught a glimpse of the Pilferer and followed him. But the part about the police van and sergeant was odd. There *might* be something in it. As soon as he could, he would take a turn down in the Victoria Street direction and see what he could smell out. He didn't really expect much, though. Och! the Pilferer had probably scarpered hours ago.

Still, that didn't prevent Angus having his ideas as to what sort of place the boy had come from. And if he was right, was there a special reason why he had chosen this particular district to hide in?

It was nearly one o'clock. In another hour Angus would go off duty. Mrs Trunket had promised roast beef and Yorkshire pudding, with fresh peas out of the garden behind the shop. Then Angus remembered that unless there had been a sudden, massive outbreak of villainy in the district, Bert Trunket would be home for dinner. That spoilt Angus's appetite, so he switched his brain to another channel, wondering if Mrs Trunket's girls and boys had recaptured the 'doos'.

Then he saw Chris Barker, pedalling along towards him with something rectangular strapped to the box on his carrier. It looked like a petrol can. It *was* a petrol can. A queer laddie, that one! Odd how, on both occasions that morning, when Angus had run into him, Chris looked as if he wanted a hole to appear in the road and swallow him up!

Why? wondered Angus. It was then that a faint suspicion dawned. Did Chris know something – something about the Pilferer that he wasn't letting on about?

'How's the pigeon hunting?' asked Angus.

'Oh . . . all right. I haven't caught any, though.'

'Have you seen young Beverley lately? She was saying she saw the Pilferer, but it was such a rigmarole I couldn't make much of it.'

'Yeah, that's Beverley all over,' nodded Chris and tried to push his bike from the kerb. Angus didn't seem to notice. He gave his helmet a tilt. There were beads of sweat under the brim. He was watching Big Annie swinging over the Maybe Site.

'They're busy today . . . especially for a Sabbath.'

'Yeah.'

'The better the day the better the deed, as my granny used to say.' Angus pondered. 'Mind you, Beverley could be right. You know, I've been giving the Pilferer a wee bit of thought.'

'Yeah?'

'Aye. It occurred to me that if he wasn't a local laddie, and that doesn't seem at all likely, then maybe he's on the run – from one of those Approved Schools say, or a Remand Home. That would account for his going to ground somewhere, wouldn't it? And Pimlico's as good a place as any. Or he may have had some reason for coming here, some notion in his head.' He eyed Chris sharply, before going on, 'If he is still around, maybe he's wanting to contact somebody in the district – somebody he daren't approach openly. Relatives, say?'

'Search me, Mr Dickie,' murmured Chris.

'Me too, laddie. I'm just chewing it over, as they say.' He smiled disarmingly. 'I'll have him – sooner or later.'

'What, because he burnt your dinner?' But Chris said that to his retreating back.

He cycled on. Wryly, he caught himself half hating Dickie Bird, now. Dickie Bird was getting clever. And he really seemed to have it in for Mousy. He was hounding him – mercilessly. Well, not really. To the policeman, Mousy was merely a challenge, a nuisance to be cleared up, a scribbled line in his notebook. To Chris he was something . . . well, much more complicated.

Dickie Bird wanted Mousy. Did Lawson, for a different reason? Chris wondered whether he'd made a new mistake; whether he should have gone straight to the Maybe Site, told Lawson where his son was, got the whole thing finished and done with. Lawson might be taking steps of his own by now. What had Mousy's stepmother told her husband? What had *he* told *her*?

Chris zig-zagged towards the basement, looking over his shoulder at frequent intervals. He wouldn't have put it past Dickie Bird to have borrowed a bike and tried to follow him, but the streets lay empty behind him.

This time Chris left his bicycle fifty yards away in an alley and lugged the petrol can the rest of the way. Mousy was playing with the cat, dangling a length of string in front of its nose. The big, sloppy creature was fooling with the string like a kitten with wool.

'I don't want a bath, mate!'

Chris flung him the soap. 'Don't drink any of the water. The can's had petrol in it.'

'Won't your dad miss the can?'

'He was killed in a motorbike accident last year.'

'Rough ... well, ta anyway.' Mousy tickled the cat's chin. 'Anything new, then?' He meant, 'have you seen my dad?'

'Not yet. I thought I'd bring you the water, first.' Chris hesitated. 'Look, Mousy, why did your dad go to prison?'

'What difference does that make?'

'I just wondered.'

'You mean the last time?' Mousy had opened the can. He was pouring water into one cupped hand, then sploshing it over his face. 'He did a bit of bird before I was born, but that was nothing. Then he teamed up with this mob. They were big time. My dad used to be a crack driver, and he drove the get-away car in a bank raid.' He told Chris all this between splashes. He might have been describing his father's prowess on the football field. 'They got shopped, though. Somebody squealed. I saw a newspaper down in Bristol, when the trial was on. Them relations tried to hide the paper, but I saw it. Front page, pictures, the works. My old man got seven years. As he's out, he must have earned remission for good conduct.'

'When did he come out?'

'Dunno. He didn't say, in his letter. Why the third degree, bonzo?'

'And now he's going straight, you said?'

'Yeah, s'far as I know.'

'What made you think he wasn't working on sites any more?'

Mousy gave him a sharp look. 'He wouldn't do that now. He's got brains, mate, and contacts. You wouldn't catch *him* hunking a lot of stones about.'

Maybe, thought Chris. He was thinking how little Mousy really knew. And Mousy, soaping his hands, brooded silently, perhaps realizing this for himself. He had his young, be-wildered look again.

Then Chris said, 'Well, I'm off.'

'To the house?' You could almost hear the cogs turn in Mousy's brain. 'Look, what's wrong with me pushing over to the house for myself? There's no need for you to run any more errands for me.'

'No!' Chris shuddered to think what might happen if Mousy turned up on his Aunt Audrey's doorstep; if she was still there. 'Let me finish the job. I've done all right so far, haven't I?'

Mousy gave in easier than Chris had expected. 'Yeah, okay bonzo, you're the boss.' But he obviously still didn't trust Chris. Perhaps trust was beyond him.

This was it, then! Next stop, Maybe Site to find Lawson who, according to Mousy's fancy, wouldn't hunk stones about nowadays. Well, perhaps he was some kind of boss man at the Site. With his clean, bright shirt he hadn't looked like a labourer. And if he was going straight, and one of his 'contacts' had got him a decent job with the contractors, he'd want to tread warily in keeping any sort of rendezvous with his absconded son. Perhaps the new job abroad, if that wasn't something cooked up in Mousy's imagination, was linked in some way with his work at the Maybe Site. Perhaps the contractors were sending him overseas to boss one of their projects. Australia? Canada?

Anyway, Chris had better be careful how he approached Lawson, or he could collect a thick ear for his trouble! Not far from the Site he caught a glimpse of Dickie Bird in the distance. He had a sudden, overwhelming impulse to ride up to him, tell him where Mousy was. Dickie Bird had a 'down' on Mousy, but he was decent. He'd see that Mousy saw his dad – if he could. But suppose he couldn't? It might not be up to him.

Chris shook his head and rode on to the Site, stopping across the street. The gate was still closed, though work continued behind the fence. The truck had gone, but Big Annie was swinging some wall sections on to the scaffolding platform high up in the partly finished building. A few bystanders gawped.

Chris banged on the gate. Nothing happened. Then he saw a man in overalls coming down the steps from a platform. The gate swung open. 'What do you want?'

'Can I see Mr Lawson?'

'What for?' The man, a middle-aged, balding figure with big, sad eyes, was giving Chris an intent look. 'He's busy.'

At least he was there! 'It's about his son, Keith. I've an important message.'

The workman shot a quick glance across Chris's shoulder into the street. 'Come through.' He shut the gate behind Chris. Then he led him to the office building. 'Wait here,'

Chris waited while the man went in. Two youths sauntered across from the scaffolding, hands in pockets, cigarettes dangling. They glanced at Chris, tapped the office door and went in. One of them was fair, like Mousy Lawson.

The workman came out, jerked his thumb towards the door and went back to the scaffolding. Chris went through the door.

Lawson wasn't in the office. Instead, a dark, thickset man with bushy eyebrows was seated at a desk. He was in shirt-sleeves. There was a pencil stuck behind his ear. 'I'm Wykes, the site manager,' he said. '*Who* did you want to see?'

'Mr Lawson.'

'Anybody with you out there?'

'No.' Chris felt three pairs of eyes on him; Wykes's, the two lounging youths'. What was going on? You could cut this atmosphere with a knife. It was almost as though his arrival had been half expected – even feared. And where was Lawson?

As if he had read Chris's thoughts, Wykes glanced at the fair youth, who went out. Nobody spoke while he was gone. Wykes wrote on a pad, ignoring Chris.

The office door opened and Lawson entered, followed by the fair youth who took up his lounging stance by a filing cabinet. Lawson looked curiously at Chris. He hadn't altered much from the figure in the snapshot; but close up, in the flesh, his eyes had a distant, chilling expression. 'All right, sonny, say your piece. What's this about Keith?'

He didn't seem to mind that the other men were listening in. Chris told his story – as much of it as necessary. He mentioned the basement, but not where it was. He would have told Lawson on his own – why else had he come? – but he didn't want anyone else to know.

He didn't yet understand, didn't know the truth, but everything about that office and its watchful, listening occupants shrieked at him to be careful what he said, how he acted.

'You followed my wife here – right?' said Lawson. It was as though he had guessed it might happen. 'Where's this photo?'

Chris still had it. He'd mentioned it in his story. He handed it over. Lawson stared at it for a long time, his cold eyes narrowed. Then he slipped it into his own pocket. 'I'll take charge of this. Where's the letter?'

'I never saw that.'

There was another silence. Chris could hear Wykes stroking his swarthy chin. The youths listened, and waited, like watchdogs. Then Lawson said, 'Well, there's one more thing you can do, sonny. Get back to Keith, wherever that place is, and tell him to beat it – beat it back to Bristol. Tell him you couldn't find me, that I've already gone away, something of the sort. Then if I was you, kid, I'd vamoozle and forget the whole thing. It's none of your affair, is it?'

'No, I guess not,' said Chris. Lawson's callousness had shaken him. But there was something else. Why had he taken the photo away? Why had he asked that guarded question about the letter he'd written Mousy? What did they matter – if he didn't even want to see Mousy? He blurted out a protest, 'Won't you even see him? He's come all the way from Bristol, risking getting caught and sent back. He's got this idea that he wants to live with you and his – his new mum . . . if you'd just talk to him . . .'

Lawson smiled, his mouth cruel. 'Not a chance, kid. Things are different, now. I'm a busy man. I can't risk having Keith on my back. Now scram, there's a good boy. My advice is not to have anything to do with Keith. He won't do you any good. You live in different worlds. Look, why don't you let him stew for a couple of hours, then tip off the police? That's your best bet.'

Sickened, Chris turned away. The darker of the two youths

caught up with him across the site, opened the gate to let him out then relocked it.

In the office the man called Wykes said, 'Was that wise – letting him go like that?'

'What did you expect me to do?' snapped Lawson. 'Bury him?'

'It's a pity your wife didn't phone, instead of leading him here.'

'I told her not to use the phone. The kid didn't suspect anything . . .' His eyes narrowed as he had a new thought. 'All the same, we'd better know where master Keith is, in case he gums things up . . . Ferdy!' The fair youth Beverley Bright had mistaken for the Pilferer looked alert. 'Get after the youngster and find out where he goes. And this time don't let any little girls scare you to death!'

Two o'clock on Sunday afternoon, and raging hot; Big Ben's twin hammer blows reverberate across the city, like an auctioneer selling off the hours.

Across the park, in Pimlico, Chris Barker is half-way back to the basement, wondering what he will tell Mousy about his dad – the dad who'd held his hand in the snapshot, the dad who now wanted him 'shopped'.

Then Chris spots the motor scooter the length of a street behind him; recognizes the front rider as the fair-headed youth from the Maybe Site. The darker man is on the pillion. So he's being followed! Why? Lawson hadn't cared where Mousy was; he hadn't asked. But now he's changed his mind and wants to know. Why? Chris nearly gives in. One glimpse of Angus's blue helmet and he'll go and spill the beans, let Mousy take his chances.

But he doesn't see Angus, because Angus has just reported off duty. The constable happens to see a circular delivered to the station that morning.

ABSCONDED FROM EVERDALE APPROVED
SCHOOL, BRISTOL
NAME: KEITH BRIAN LAWSON   AGED 13 4/12
DESCRIPTION...
BELIEVED TO BE MAKING FOR SOUTH-WEST LONDON
AREA ... etc. etc.

'Och!' mutters Angus. 'That's the laddie. That's him!'

Chris heads away from the basement and rides towards the pigeon lofts instead. But as Chris makes for the outer stairs, the youths' figures come leaping after him like shapes in a shadow show.

Mousy sweats in his garden. The insects drone. The cat is asleep on the brick wall. Mousy is waiting for Chris to come back, but Chris has been gone a long time and Mousy's suspicious mind has a canker of doubt in it: will Chris shop him after all?

Beverley and Connie are at the lofts and Connie has put the little brown puppy in one of the empty nesting boxes; and Beverley is worried twice. Once because Connie is getting much too attached to the pup; the way she is mothering it she obviously expects to keep it for ever. Twice because she hasn't seen the Chans for hours. Where can they be?

Bruce and Sidney have disappeared, leaving no clue to their whereabouts except Monsieur Poirot's pigeon basket on the underground station platform. And the Chans ... all four of them are stretched out on the grass by the lake in St James's Park, doing absolutely nothing.

Around them the city is awhirl with activity, and drama, and lost pigeons, and people; peanut sellers and ice-cream sellers and postcard sellers; people feeding the ducks and pelicans and trying to feed the Life-Guards' horses; photographers, picnickers and tennis players. But three of the Chans have their eyes shut and their heads rested on linked hands behind them.

Their legs are crossed like effigies of knights on tombs. Only Jimmy Chan is sitting up and that is because he has the bird cage and in the cage, cooing contentedly and drowsily, are two of the doped pigeons: Pigeon Oswald, an albino, and Pigeon David, the little cobbie. Jimmy is looking after the pigeons.

Quite a lot of fuss was made, earlier, when Heather Chan was got out of the lake. Some bathers from Hyde Park happened to be going by and they lent towels. Someone suggested taking the wet Chans home in a car but by then Leo was back with the cobbie from the islet, and Lena, steaming wet, was bringing Jimmy by the hand from the direction of Horseguards' Parade.

'It's okay, really,' said Leo Chan. 'The sun will dry us. Presently we'll lie down in the sun and it will dry us. We're looking for pigeons.' A largish crowd had gathered by now, and at the front was the polka-dot girl who had the most to say.

'So that's why you all got into the lake? Oh, my!'

'Yes, we have two pigeons now,' said Leo, 'because our brother Jimmy has found one and I've got the other. Look!' He held the cobbie up for all to see. With his wet hands he kept the pigeon's wings pinioned and tipped him a little to one side so that the people could see the ring on his foot. 'You see that ring on his foot? Well, that means he's a racing-pigeon and he's pretty valuable.'

'How many of them got loose?' asked the polka-dot girl.

'Six,' said Leo, beaming. 'We've got two, so that makes four to go. They've all got these rings round their feet.'

The crowd got bigger because, from a distance, it looked as though Leo was selling something. The polka-dot girl said, '*We* used to keep pigeons, once. We live by the sea. One day one of ours ate some shoe polish and do you know what happened?'

The crowd shook their heads.

'Well, we never saw it again. My dad said it must have flown out to sea. Can you imagine?'

The crowd shook their heads again. 'Well,' said the polka-dot girl. 'Who's for pigeons? Hands up those who'll help look for the lost pigeons?'

A lot of hands went up. Most of them were children's, but not all. 'Jolly good!' said the polka-dot girl. She waved at the Chans. 'You'll be all right till we get back? We'll search the

park from end to end. If you've found two pigeons the rest are probably not far away.'

The Chans waved to the crowd, who waved back then began faning out in all directions across the park. Leo, Lena and Heather stretched out on the grass leaving Jimmy to sit by the cage. First they lay on their faces and their backs steamed gently until they were dry, then they began to toast. One by one they turned over and their fronts steamed and toasted in turn, but all this took a long time and Jimmy had nothing to do because he wasn't wet.

Presently he looked at the others trying to guess whether they were asleep or not. He nudged Leo with his toe but Leo only snorted and went on steaming. Jimmy got up and crept away to a van selling crisps and, when he came back, he fed himself and, at the same time, he fed the wild birds. He had more sense than to feed Monsieur Poirot's pigeons with the crisps. They still had a little of Bruce Roper's grain for that.

Several birds alighted near Jimmy, waiting for bits of crisp. First came the sparrows who started pecking up the crumbs. Then some starlings flew down from the trees, and their big spotty bodies took over, nudging the sparrows away. Last of all came the wild pigeons with their fatter-still, big-bully bodies and they nudged the starlings.

Jimmy Chan remembered what the old gentleman had told him in Trafalgar Square – or he *thought* he remembered. 'These are *something* pigeons, and they're descended from *something*, and that's why . . .'

Pigeon Oswald and Pigeon David were dozing off, squeezed up against each other on the floor of the cage. Jimmy reached out a foot and nudged the cage. The bell tinkled and the pigeons woke up and made throaty noises like rusty sewing machines.

And then Big Ben struck two and the polka-dot girl ran from across the park and said, excitedly, 'I say, wake up you kids! We've seen pigeons – two more of them, maybe three. They seem to be heading somewhere – somewhere across the lake towards those buildings over there!'

Leo sat up. 'Pimlico!' he said. 'They can't be . . .?'

'Heading for home, flying back to the lofts?' said Lena.

'*Can't* be!' said Leo huskily. 'Come on, let's go and see.' He explained to the polka-dot girl just where Monsieur Poirot's lofts were and what he and Lena had guessed.

'Well, I hope you're right,' said the polka-dot girl. 'I'd love to come with you, but I'd better stay here and look after the troops! They're a keen lot, but we want to keep them on their toes, don't we? We haven't actually *caught* the pigeons yet. Well, cheerio.'

And she was gone, her pretty eyes sparkling with enthusiasm.

11 Arrest?

Chris had panicked a little. On top of everything else that had happened, the skin-crawling sensation of being hounded by the two youths from the Maybe Site drove him into hasty action.

Vaguely he had thought of Bruce Roper. Solid, dependable Bruce would help, because Chris would tell him everything, now. He'd expected to find Bruce at the lofts, but instead there were only Beverley Bright and her kid sister, messing about with that puppy they'd found.

'Where's Bruce?' demanded Chris.

'He went off ages ago with Sidney. I'm looking after the lofts. What's happened? You're as white as a sheet.'

Chris didn't answer. He turned, darted across to the loft structure nearest the street and peered down, cautiously. The youths were lounging in a doorway, pretending not to look in his direction. Lawson must have sent them. Because he wanted to know where Mousy was, after all? And he could only find that out by having Chris followed. The youths must be puzzled, though. Chris had mentioned a basement, and they could see there was no basement here.

Suddenly the fair one, a bit like Mousy, said something to his companion, shot a quick look at the Poirots' house, then ran off round the corner. Chris heard the scooter start up. That was when Beverley joined him – after the fair youth had gone. Chris guessed that he was either going to ride back to the Maybe Site, or find a telephone kiosk, make his report, and ask for fresh instructions.

Beverley said, 'What are you looking at? Why won't you say what's going on?'

Mousy was waiting – waiting for Chris to come back with a message from his father. If the message didn't arrive, he might get impatient and do something stupid. Yet if Chris went to the basement now, the youths would follow him. There was no way of eluding them – they had the scooter. Unless Chris made a dart for it now, while the fair-haired one wasn't there ... no, too risky. He'd probably be back in a minute.

Chris said, 'Beverley I want you to run a message. I'll look after Connie.'

Beverley frowned doubtfully. 'Okay, but where – and why?'

'I can't explain now. You've got to trust me – I know what I'm doing. You see that dark chap across the street? Don't stick your head out!'

'I see him. He keeps looking up this way.'

'There were a couple of them,' said Chris. He knew he would have to tell Beverley part of it – that was only fair. The trouble was she could be such a muddle-head! 'They're following me. They want to know where somebody is. I've got to tell him something – the person who's hiding – but if I go to him they'll follow. They've got a scooter.'

'But who's hiding – and why?'

'That boy Dickie Bird is after.'

'The Pimlico Pilferer! You want me to go to *him*?'

Chris was losing patience. 'Look, this morning you thought you were chasing him, and you seemed to be enjoying it. You weren't scared then.'

'I'm not scared, only ... only you said he's got a knife and ...'

'Oh, I only *said* that, to put you off. He isn't violent ...'

Then Chris remembered the savage attack Mousy had made on him at their first meeting. But surely even Mousy wouldn't behave like that to a girl? He said, 'I'm going to tell you where the place is, so listen. When you get there, don't creep about and frighten him. Call his name, only quietly. Tell him I sent you. He's to stay put until I come. Warn him that some men are looking for him, so he'd better keep his head down ...'

There were other details, and directions for getting to the basement, and Chris could see that Beverley was trying hard not to ask anything else. He said, 'I think that's all. Is your bike here?'

'No. Can I borrow yours?'

'Can't be done – they may recognize it. The point of this is that they don't know you, so they won't follow – so long as you don't actually stare at them in the street. Anything else?'

'When you say some men are after the Pilferer, do you mean *policemen*?'

'No, and that's the last question I'm answering till you come back. Get moving, *please!* If you've still got that daft old saucepan you'd better take that and pretend to look for pigeons. That'll fox them!'

'Okay,' said Beverley. She produced a mock shudder. 'If I don't come back, you'll know I've been cut up in little pieces. Don't let Connie maul the puppy about too much.'

She fetched the saucepan, went down the steps, and marched off along the street, willing herself not to look at the dark youth in the doorway.

But it was his companion, coming back on the scooter, who spotted her leaving the Poirots' house. If it hadn't been for the saucepan, thrust rather deliberately out in front of her, he might not have recognized her. But that did it. Ferdy didn't believe in coincidences. Ever since it had happened, he'd been puzzling his head as to why that girl and the little one had dogged his steps practically all the way to the garage behind the Maybe Site, where he had gone on a message for Lawson. Now they – or at least, the one with the saucepan – had turned up again. Hadn't she just come from that house with the flat roof? It didn't take a genius to guess that she was in some way connected with the kid who had called at the site about Lawson's son. Anyway, she might be worth keeping track of.

Ferdy turned his scooter and cruised very slowly a sensible distance behind the girl. Even if she looked round, she wouldn't recognize him – unless of course she'd seen him across the street from the house. Ferdy was wearing goggles.

Beverley reached the basement, identifying it by Chris's careful directions. She hung back for a few moments, gingerly looking at those curtained windows. Did the curtains move a little? She couldn't be sure.

An old lady lived there, Chris had said, but she didn't appear to know that Mousy had been hiding in her basement since Saturday morning. Mousy – that was the name she was to call, when she got down to the broken window. 'Don't frighten him,' Chris had said.

She blinked once more at the upper windows, then began going down the steps. She left the saucepan half-way down and was about to complete her descent when she happened to look through the railings – and her heart seemed to turn over. The scooter was gliding past with its engine switched off. The fair youth was looking towards her and his goggles were raised.

The Pimlico Pilferer! No, of course it wasn't; Chris said the pilferer was a boy from an approved school called Mousy. *He* was hiding in the basement. In that case, why had this youth tried to avoid her?

Beverley lost her head, scrambled up the steps and ran – ran blindly, senselessly through the sun-drenched streets.

Chris Barker stared unsympathetically at the sobbing figure by the lofts. 'But you should have gone on and warned Mousy. All you did was show that chap what he wanted to know. You couldn't have made it clearer if you'd chalked it on the pavement in letters six feet high.'

'My brain played tricks.'

'Your *what?*' said Chris, unkindly.

'I thought perhaps if I moved quickly enough, he wouldn't notice that I'd gone down the steps,' said Beverley, but she knew this was absurd. She'd just acted instinctively, and her instinct happened to be wrong! 'You didn't tell me *he* was the other chap, besides the dark one.'

'How could I know he was the one you hared after this morning? All I know is that he works at the Maybe Site, where Mousy's father is. I'll tell you about that later. Do you reckon he followed you back?'

'Not unless he has wings,' sniffed Beverley. 'I practically flew. I cut through alleys and things.'

Chris looked down from the roof. The dark youth had gone some time ago, perhaps wondering what had happened to his pal. The absence of both of them made Chris feel more uneasy than their skulking presence had done. He didn't believe that the fair youth couldn't have followed Beverley if he'd wanted to. Of course, there was no need! He knew where Mousy was, now, and he'd have told Lawson. What was Lawson doing about it?

'Where are you going?' asked Beverley, as Chris made off.

'To the basement. And if *I* don't come back, you'd better send for the Flying Squad!'

Chris was sure nobody followed him this time. He stood on his pedals and ripped the shortest way to the basement. On the journey a secret voice seemed to whisper, 'So they've probably got Mousy. Why should *you* care?'

Chris didn't know the answer. All he knew was that he *cared*. But as soon as he reached the steps, and saw the monstrous old cat rubbing its scrawny back against the railings, he knew that Mousy had gone. Beverley's saucepan lay abandoned at the bottom. The gap through the broken window had been widened: bits of the rotten frame were scattered over the area. Chris crawled through into the garden, past the spilled bags of rotten rags, and a smashed and upended chair.

Mousy must have put up quite a fight. Of course, he *would* have. But in the garden there were few signs of his habitation. Chris found the petrol can, and the medicine bottle in which he'd brought the milk; and a clothes brush, stuck end up in the weeds.

A voice above Chris said, 'Hey! What's going on now? Who are you?'

Chris looked up, startled. An old man with bent shoulders was glaring at him from the little landing atop the steps. He wore a grubby pinafore round his middle and he had been doing something with the frying pan in his hand. There was a deaf-aid in his ear. 'If you're looking for your mate, he's gorn,' said the old man. 'Some coppers just come and fetched him. They had a van. I never knew he was there.'

'A van?' said Chris.

'Eh? Oh, yes – a blue van.' For some reason he looked annoyed. He wasn't even grousing at Chris for being in his garden. 'Mate of yours, was he? Well, I don't know what he'd done, but them policemen didn't half lay into him. Mind you, he gave as good as he got, considering his size. Fought like a tiger, he did.' His eyes looked admiring, then angry again. 'If I'd been forty years younger I'd have landed into that sergeant bloke myself, and chanced the consequences. He was the one who was roughest on your mate. And when I came out and

asked him what he meant by busting my basement windows, without a word of apology, he said things I daren't repeat! And he calls himself a policeman! They got no consideration for us old folks, living on our own – not these days they haven't. Well, *most* coppers are good-hearted enough, but that sergeant ... lummy, the way he dragged your mate up them steps you'd think he'd committed triple murder at least. I dunno what the world's coming to ...'

He went on letting off steam, but Chris wasn't listening any more. He was remembering what Beverley Bright had said; about the police sergeant and another policeman, and a van. About having followed the fair-haired youth to a garage behind the Maybe Site; the youth who'd turned out to be some kind of messenger boy of Lawson's – or Wykes's, the site manager.

Could the youth have been on his way to the garage when Beverley had pursued him? And if so, was that why he'd been so keen to shake her off?

And had Mousy *really* been arrested?

At three o'clock the Chans were coming back into Pimlico, leaving the Polka-dot girl and her 'troops' searching the park. The Chans all felt pretty good, because they had caught two pigeons. Across Birdcage Walk, Leo said, 'We'll take these back to the lofts, then we'll return to the park and help look for some more.'

'That's what *I* was going to say,' said Lena Chan.

Jimmy was still carrying the cage, but his arm was aching. Two pigeons were heavier than one. He tried his other arm, but that ached, too. He lagged behind Leo and Lena, and Heather lagged behind Jimmy because she'd walk a little way then suddenly dance round in a circle.

'Hey!' said Jimmy. '*You* carry the cage.'

Heather took the cage from Jimmy. Jimmy ran on to catch

up the others. Heather lagged farther behind still because her arm was weaker than Jimmy's, so it ached even sooner.

By and by, she put the cage down on the pavement – so suddenly that a pedestrian just behind almost tripped over it. Pigeon Oswald and Pigeon David sat side by side, still staring at one another in a dazed, astonished way – like two astronauts unexpectedly finding themselves in the same space capsule.

But something else odd had happened. Heather's almond eyes widened and she set the cage down. Then she crouched beside it and peered at the sawdust in the bottom. Heather saw the Thing lying there, sparkling white, in the sawdust next to the little seed bowl. She didn't know when it had happened but one of them, Pigeon Oswald or Pigeon David, had laid an egg!

Heather had never seen such a *small* real egg in her life. And so white, so beautiful. She wanted to hold the egg in her hand for a moment. She had never held such an egg before. She sat cross-legged on the side of the pavement, and people looked at her but she didn't see them. All she saw was the egg. She started to remove the side of the cage because she couldn't quite reach the egg through the proper little door. She got the egg all right, and was holding it, but the side of the cage fell away from its rusty old grooves. And the pigeons took off! Away they went, beating their suddenly strong wings, crazy with freedom.

Lena looked round and shrieked. Leo looked round and came running back. '*You!*' said Leo. 'You . . . you . . . you . . .'

They all stared into the brightness of the sky above the buildings – stared until their eyes watered and that wasn't altogether the brightness. But the pigeons had vanished.

Leo said, 'Oh, well, we might as well go back to the lofts, anyway.'

'Yes,' sighed Lena. 'We'd better see if the others have had any luck. Jimmy, bring the . . .' But she couldn't say any more. She wasn't even interested in the pigeon egg.

At the lofts, they found Connie poking at a cat with the bean pole and Beverley Bright squatting on a basket with her chin miserably in her hands. Connie put the pole down and took the Chans across to see the puppy in his temporary home.

Lena came back to Beverley and asked, 'What's up, Beverley? Haven't you caught any pigeons?'

'One,' said Beverley, 'but Connie lost it.' She didn't explain why she was *really* miserable.

'*Two*,' groaned Lena Chan, 'but our Heather let them *both* go.'

They thought it was Bruce coming up the stairs, but it wasn't. It was Chris Barker, and none of them had ever seen him look so much like a ghost of himself. He flung himself down, listened silently to the chatter for a few minutes, then he said, 'Oh, shut up! Shut up about pigeons. Something more serious has happened. Beverley knows part of it, but I want to tell it all, from the beginning, then I want you to help.'

'Sure, Chris,' nodded Leo Chan. He didn't really believe it, but he thought he saw tears in Chris's eyes.

They sat around anywhere they could, watching Chris's face until he couldn't bear it any longer and pretended to blow his nose. The younger children, sensing that this was going to be older-brother-and-sister talk, crept away to amuse themselves with Connie's puppy in the old nesting-box.

The shadows of the lofts were beginning to lengthen, but it was still only mid-afternoon. And no dinner! Nobody had noticed the time. Nobody was worrying about angry and anxious parents.

Chris told them everything he knew, everything he guessed. It was a long and complex story, especially with the guesses, but his mind was vivid with so many memories that he had kept pent up till now.

Out the story poured. In a way, they all met Mousy Lawson with his bragging and longing and mistrusting. They crouched with him in the insect-infested basement garden, felt the ants crawl on their clothes. They met the painted face of Mousy's stepmother in Petit Cochon Street, and watched the muscles ripple on Lawson's powerful arms. They tried to imagine their own ordinary, kindly fathers saying, 'I don't want you on my back!' – and meaning it. They felt the brutal police sergeant grasp their clothing and drag them, bouncing, up those basement steps.

And when it was all over, Chris looked more dejected than ever and said, half in challenge, 'Well, go on! Tell me what an idiot I've been. Tell me I should have shopped Mousy the first chance I got, before I had time to think. Tell me!'

But there was a long silence.

Then Leo said, quietly, 'No, Chris. You did what you thought was right. And you did *something*. It's nearly always better to do something than nothing. I mean, you could have just gone off and left Mousy alone.' He laughed awkwardly. 'I think I might have done that.'

'No you wouldn't!' said Lena, loyally. 'Look what you did at the lake. You would have done just what Chris did. Maybe we all would have.'

'Not me!' smiled Beverley, but not with her eyes. 'I'd have just got everything in a muddle as usual.'

But it wasn't what they all might have done, but what they had to do now. Leo took the lead, this time. 'I think as Chris thinks. Lawson's still a crook. And he's *planning* something. The fair chap Beverley thought was the Pilferer is one of his men, and so is the dark one. But I don't think they're important ...'

'What about those policemen who were hiding in the garage?' asked Lena. 'Do you think Chris is right: that they aren't real policemen at all?'

Leo shrugged. 'They don't sound real – the way they treated Mousy and spoke to that old man. And it was a bit of a coincidence that they turned up soon after Beverley had accidentally shown the fair chap the basement.'

'Then Mousy hasn't been arrested at all!' gasped Lena Chan. 'He's been – been . . . what's the word?'

'Abducted,' said Chris. 'And Lawson must have organized it, so the bogus cops *are* in his gang. What I don't get, though, is why he didn't try and find out from me where his son was hiding.'

Leo had an answer to that. 'Either he changed his mind, or he didn't want you to know that he meant to abduct Mousy.' He thought this last point over. 'He's scared of Mousy, that's what it is; scared in case his own son somehow gives him away to the real police. Perhaps Lawson said something important in that letter he wrote. He seemed jolly keen to know whether Chris had it or not, didn't he Chris?'

'Maybe,' said Chris. 'But in any case if Lawson has a crime planned – something coming off soon – then Mousy being on the loose would be bound to worry him. I reckon that's why he sent the fake policemen after him. It was clever, though a bit dangerous – having to drive that van across Victoria Street, for instance. Suppose the real cops saw it and knew it shouldn't be there? Lawson must have been pretty desperate . . .'

'And I bet that means the crime's due to happen soon — perhaps even today!'

'At the Maybe Site?' said Beverley. 'But what crime could they commit there? It's only a lot of holes and bricks and things.'

'We'd better warn the police,' said Leo.

But Chris laughed hopelessly. 'About what? Don't you think I would have done that already if I thought it would work? They wouldn't believe us. We haven't any proof that anything *is* going to happen. They'd say we'd made it all up . . .'

'Unless,' added Leo, solemnly, 'we could produce the Pimlico Pilferer. Mousy might know more than he told you . . .'

Chris glowered. Leo shrugged, smiled, and went on, 'Okay, I know you don't want that, Chris. Where do you reckon Mousy is?'

'I've been wondering that. If the bogus police are still using the garage place as a sort of base they may have taken him there. I'm going down there ...' He grinned sheepishly. 'I'm not saying I'll do anything spectacular even if I get the chance, but ... well, Mousy might think I shopped him and I'm not having that if I can help it.'

'I'll come with you,' said Leo, making up his mind quickly.

'What about us?' asked Lena.

Chris said, 'See if you can find Dickie Bird. He may believe you. But don't tell him where Leo and I have gone, or he may nab Mousy before we get a chance to do anything.'

Lena nodded. 'I think he'll be gone off duty by now, but we could go to Mrs Trunket's. Maybe Bert Trunket's there, too, and Bert's a real Scotland Yard detective!'

'Do be careful, Chris – and Leo,' said Beverley.

Chris smiled, but not very cheerfully. 'There's only one thing I'm really scared of, and that's what Mousy will do when he finds out that his dad doesn't want him – doesn't even want to *see* him!'

Then, leaving Jimmy in charge of the lofts and the younger children, they set out down the roof stairs.

12 Escape

When Angus got to his lodgings, Mrs Trunket asked, 'Have you found the Pilferer yet?'

'No, but I've found out a wee bit about him.'

Angus described the circular he'd seen at the police station. Mrs Trunket tut-tutted. 'Poor little scrap. I expect he's never had a chance.'

'I dinna ken women,' said Angus, putting on his accent. 'Yesterday you thought boiling in oil was too good for him.'

'What have you got on this afternoon?' asked Mrs Trunket, delicately trying to change the subject.

'Duty! Oh, aye, I won't be wearing my uniform, but they can't stop me staying on the job if I want. There's funny business going on in Pimlico today, for a Sabbath. Did you know about the pigeons?'

Mrs Trunket hadn't heard about them, so Angus put his helmet on Bert Trunket's chair, loosened his tie, and said, 'Weel, your lasses and laddies are all out looking for the doos that got away from the Poirots' lofts this morning. They've got a cage, and a tool box and even an old saucepan. Och! Kids! By the way, what sort of laddie is that Chris?'

'Chris Barker?' Mrs Trunket thought as she laid out knives, forks and spoons. 'A good boy, I'd say. Very willing and honest, if a shade on the moody side. Lost his dad last year, not long before you came. Why, what's he done?'

'I don't know yet. Honest, you say? Aye, weel, could be. But he knows something he won't tell, and it's my opinion it has something to do with the lad from the Approved School.'

'How do you make that out?' Mrs Trunket frowned. 'I'm not saying that, in certain circumstances, Chris *wouldn't* help a boy like that. It would depend.' But she didn't say on what.

'Anyway,' said Angus, 'I'll be pursuing certain lines of inquiry this afternoon – just on my own initiative.'

Bert Trunket came down from his room, picked up Angus's helmet and pointedly placed it on the sideboard. 'Hi, Jock!'

'Good afternoon,' said Angus. He hated to be called 'Jock'.

'What's this about lines of inquiry?' asked the C.I.D. man. 'Still after a plain clothes job with us, are you, Jock?'

Bert Trunket had a reddish, grinning face, and Angus would often have punched his nose if he hadn't liked Mrs Trunket and found his lodgings comfortable. All the same, Angus swallowed his pride that day because, whatever his faults, Bert Trunket was a mine of information on police matters. Angus took some of his confidence with a pinch of salt, of course. For instance a detective constable could scarcely be on quite such intimate terms with senior officers of Scotland Yard as Bert was inclined to suggest. It was also one of his little conceits that he aped the voice and gestures of his hero, Chief Superintendent Barlow.

'Do your people know anything about an absconded boy from Bristol, name of Keith Lawson?' inquired Angus, and he was gratified to see Bert's face go blank. Angus hadn't wanted Bert to know. The Pimlico Pilferer was *his* case.

'We leave runaway kids to the uniformed branch,' shrugged the detective. He added, infuriatingly, 'Or the women police...'

and broke off. '*What* did you say his name was again?' Angus repeated it.

'Lawson? Well, it must be a coincidence.'

'*What's* a coincidence?'

'That would be telling, Jock, boy!'

Angus bristled. 'Look, man, I'm as much a copper as you, and don't you forget it! Don't always be treating me like a kid of six. I've been sweating it out since yesterday, looking all over Pimlico for this absconder, and if you know something about him why the dickens don't you say so? Isn't there to be just a wee bit of cooperation between the C.I.D. and us uniformed men?' Angus suddenly thought of something else. 'That police van . . . I suppose you wouldn't know about that. Would you?'

'Now then, you two!' said Mrs Trunket, entering with the food. 'Let's have no fighting.'

But now Bert Trunket was definitely puzzled. Even the almost permanent grin had vanished. 'What are you talking about?'

'Och! According to my information there's been a police van stowed away in some garage across from the Maybe Site. There's a uniformed sergeant in charge. Do they really need a police van to collect a poor, wee scrap like Keith Lawson?'

'I don't know about that, Jock,' admitted Bert, reluctantly. 'If the motorized police are out in Pimlico today, that's something they didn't tell me.' He went on, trying to placate Angus, 'Lawson happens to be a crook with a record as long as a street. He's moved back into the district recently and is making our blokes scratch their heads, see? We think he's got something up his sleeve. He's taken up with the foreman of the Maybe Site, a shifty character called Wykes, and has some sort of job with the contractors we can't quite figure. But it's him we're watching, not some runaway kid from Bristol. So far as I'm concerned, Jock boy, you can catch all the absconders you like, do them up in bags and sell them off two a penny. Now do you mind passing the salt?'

Mousy was sure who had shopped him. The policeman had told him – that rotten bully of a sergeant who'd dragged him by his arm up the steps and bundled him into the van. 'Who shopped me; that Chris something?'

'Yeah ... yeah,' the sergeant had said, taciturnly. 'He did.' Mousy brooded on that. He had started to think Chris on the level. Had all that to-ing and fro-ing just been an elaborate, long-drawn-out game of some sort? Had Chris only pretended to find the house, to be contacting his dad, just to keep Mousy pinned in the basement until the police had time to fetch him?

Mousy didn't know. He shrugged away the emptiness and disappointment and filled himself with new hate. Bonzo! If he ever got the chance he would 'do' that Chris! He was pretty sure this rotten rozzer wouldn't let him see his dad before shipping him back to Bristol. If he did, look out, mate! His dad would fix that bullying copper, once and for all.

The van braked, swerved off the road, and they were in some hollow-sounding building with the motor bleating for a moment before it was killed. The rough hands grabbed him again, pushed him through a doorway, and a lock clicked. Mousy found himself in a dusty, sweltering room, about ten feet square, with a single slot of window high up at the top. The room was bare, except for some broken old office furniture and a couple of heavy lorry tyes. The floor was littered with rubbish.

That was when suspicions came crowding in for the first time. This place wasn't any police station! Mousy knew what they were like, all right. And he knew coppers, too. They could be nasty up to a point, if you turned nasty with them. But mostly they came the kind uncle stuff, and gave you biscuits, and preached a bit. They didn't push you around without a word, half break your arm, then lock you up in a dirty room.

Mousy realized that he hadn't even been searched. He still had his haversack, the socks he'd never got round to changing, his dad's letter – and the map of London. He read the letter through, but it didn't make much sense any more and it just made him feel empty and miserable so he thrust it back into his pocket.

Chris hadn't returned the snapshot, but Mousy had the map. If he could somehow get out of this dump and make it across to his old home, maybe he'd see his dad after all. Or his Aunt Audrey. Then maybe he'd find out what was going on and who these so-called coppers were . . .

Mousy looked round, his eyes taking in the furniture, the dusty strip of high window. Yeah, he'd got out of tighter spots than this in his time.

It took a while for Mousy to organize his escape, piling up the furniture – slowly, bit by bit, so as not to make any un-necessary noise – until he had built a platform high enough to enable him to reach the window. After that he had to climb up on his rickety tower just as carefully, because he had just this one chance. If the bogus police caught him trying to make a getaway they'd make sure it didn't happen again.

It stayed pretty quiet in the garage, but sometimes the voices of the men filtered through unintelligibly, and once the engine of the van sprang to life for an instant before dying away.

Reaching the window was easy enough and so was pushing it half open against its stiff, rusty fastenings – it opened horizon-tally along its entire length. Getting through would be a squeeze but Mousy reckoned he could manage that all right. What wasn't going to be so simple was reaching the ground outside in one piece; it was a good twelve feet down to the top of a brick wall studded with bottle-glass. The wall he was look-ing down at (the side of the garage) was built up against the bricks, and there were another seven or eight feet to go into a concrete-paved alley dividing the buildings. Mousy could see no sort of handhold on the way down – certainly none he could reach from his present position.

He pushed his head further through the shallow gap of the opened window, but could see only unending rooftops and windows of dingy buildings, faced with wire-netting and steel grids. When he twisted his neck and looked up, he saw over to his right the huge, slewing jib of a monster crane with a large wall panel of some kind attached to its chain pick-up. He could hear the crane's motor above the hum of traffic far away; but here, apart from the occasional sounds in the garage, it was almost eerily quiet.

Mousy grasped the window frame and began heaving himself through, taking the weight of his body on his arms. Fury was welling up inside him, now – fury that he could get out of the window but not down. For a single, crazy second he was tempted to push himself right through, take his chance on landing down there with no bones broken, without ripping himself to pieces on the jagged wall-glass. Then he cursed himself for an idiot and began lowering himself back on to his furniture platform. He would have to think of some way, that was all . . .

Then suddenly two boys appeared along the alley. One of them was a plump, Chinese-looking kid; the other was Chris! They were both looking up at the garage window – they'd seen him, but they had more sense than to yell. They came immediately below the spot where Mousy clung, a short whispered conference took place, then the Chinese kid crossed the alley into a yard filled with all kinds of junk. Mousy couldn't see him after that but apparently he beckoned to Chris, because Chris went in, too. A moment later they came out again, carrying between them a long, stout, wooden scaffolding pole. They set this against the wall under the window and it reached with some of its length to spare. No signals were necessary between

the three of them – Mousy simply heaved himself through, twisted himself nimbly on to the pole while the other boys held it secure below, then slithered down. They didn't stop to remove the pole but ran, without speaking, along the alley until they could duck into the first available shelter. This happened to be a dilapidated wooden garage letting on to a driveway at the alley's end.

Leo pulled the door to and they sat just inside on some cans and tyres, panting in the gloom. Chris felt Mousy's gaze on his face. Once Mousy had realized that the policemen weren't genuine – that he hadn't really been arrested – there was no reason why he should have gone on thinking that Chris had 'shopped' him. Yet in a confused, unreasonable way he still didn't trust Chris – he didn't trust either of his rescuers.

He didn't thank them, either! He only sniffed contemptuously when Chris explained that he thought the men with the police van had been masquerading. 'Tell us something new, mate!' They had to listen to long strings of not very choice language regarding what he thought of the 'sergeant' and what he would do to him if he ever got the chance.

He went on and on about what had happened to him, but he didn't ask the question Chris was expecting: what did my dad say? Have you found my dad? Then Chris sensed there was a reason. Mousy had had time to think; not much, but enough. Mousy, who was no fool, must have wondered whether there was any connection between his bogus 'arrest' and the fact that his father was – or had been – a crook. It must all have been pretty baffling, but surely he had made guesses, asked himself questions? *Or was he incapable of facing the truth?*

Chris knew he would have to tell him – now. There was no possible alternative. When they left their temporary shelter they would have to go somewhere, do something – something that had a connection, a working out, with all they had said and shared since morning.

So when Mousy dried up at last, Chris let him have it – straight, without useless preamble. 'Mousy, we think it was your dad who put them on to you – the men in police uniforms.'

In the semi-darkness Mousy tensed: a narrow streak of sunlight from the door slashed his face, making it hideous. 'Come again?'

'We're only guessing – most of it. It seems likely he's planning a job, a crime, and when you turned up you scared him. You might have . . . got in the way, something like that. So he sent some of his gang after you . . .'

'Just a minute, bonzo – you *are* guessing. You haven't even met my old man.'

'I have, Mousy. He's working at the building site – the Maybe Site, we call it. The one with the big crane . . . you can see it from outside. I met him – never mind how. He doesn't want you, Mousy. He told me . . . he even tried to make me squeal on you to the real police. He said, "Tell him to beat it back to Bristol!" He even took that photo away, and he was worried about the letter he'd written. I'm not saying he wanted to hurt you, but . . .'

'Dirty liar!' The words were spat out of the shadows. 'Do you expect me to believe all that? My own dad, tell *you* to shop *me*? Who're you kidding, mate? *I* know why he sent them dummy coppers to fetch me. It was so I'd be safe – safe from the law, safe from grassing, lying so-and-so's like you and this slant-eyed kid you've brought with you. Maybe he has got a job on, and good luck to him. He wants me with him, and he chose that way of doing it. Out of my way, Bonzo!'

Chris felt the fist smash into his face, and he reeled backwards against the wall of the garage. He heard the door fling open, Leo gasp, Mousy's footsteps pound along the alley. He did not try to follow. Mousy had put himself out of reach. What was it Lawson had said? 'You live in different worlds.'

'Are you okay, Leo?'

'Yeah ... he half choked me, but ... yeah.' They were out-side in the deserted alley. Leo said, 'Where do you think he's gone now?'

Chris blinked up at Big Annie's swinging jib as it appeared over the derelict roofs. 'The Maybe Site – and Lawson,' he said. 'He's going to get the truth – the hard way.'

Nearly four o'clock at the Maybe Site and the gate was still secured and the knots of spectators were still watching the work in progress. Big Annie was finished with the prefabrications from the lorries and now she was dipping and slewing across the huge site itself. Apparently while the restive and argu-mentative workmen were briefly on the scene, and earning double time for Sunday, orders had been given to remove a mountainous pile of tarpaulin-wrapped crates from a situation near the central footings to the far side beyond the lofty, scaffolded section of the new building.

It was fascinating to watch; the crates were bulky, but Big Annie tossed them skywards with the ease and skill of an angler fishing for minnows. The man in the little box high up on her cross-girders was more like a very small ant on a very large roundabout.

Lawson stood outside the office building, smoking, remem-bering. Years ago he had been employed on this very site, demolishing the old buildings that had stood here. Some of the workmen had made a very curious discovery. Deep below the foundations, they'd discovered a network of old shafts and tunnels. Sewers? Access points to the underground railway? Lawson had never inquired – it hardly mattered. A few of the men had explored down there, and one of them made a joke. 'I reckon with a few sticks of dynamite you could get clean through into the vaults of the bank!' It had been only a joke. The man had forgotten it.

Lawson remembered. It started as a crazy dream but while he was serving his long term of imprisonment, it became a plan. He was lucky, and industrious. In prison he met men with know-how, men who would help – at a price. From time to time he learned of the labour troubles at the Maybe Site. When he was released, he discovered that work was still going on; it was still possible to get into those tunnels.

It took a lot of thought, a great deal of scheming and bribing and cajoling. But Lawson was determined and a good 'fixer'. It helped a lot when he met Wykes and found him to be 'bent' – bent enough, anyway, to come in as partner with forty per cent takings. The takings would be big.

It was to be daylight robbery. The crane bit, and the bit with the bogus police and their 'borrowed' van – these were rather fancy, Lawson admitted. But at night, the area and the bank were thick with guards – and coppers. Suspicious coppers, who had been watching Lawson, wondering about Lawson. He knew that. So you had to be subtle, and fancy, and . . . *different*.

Lawson lit a fresh cigarette from the stub of the old one and thought of his son, Keith. It was just his luck that the little so-and-so should skedaddle from that school and come down here looking for him; this week-end of all times! Maybe he shouldn't have written that letter; not that he'd given anything away in it, had he? And if he'd gone abroad without writing, and Keith had kicked up a shindy and gone whining to the authorities, there might have been awkward inquiries – very awkward.

Still, it was all okay now. Audrey had warned him – told him Keith had got some youngster running messages for him. What Wykes had said was true, of course – he couldn't have left it to that kid to do the right thing, at the right time. So he'd had that brainwave and sent the boys from Sector B – the garage – to fix Keith. All in all, Lawson didn't feel he'd handled things too badly. He'd taken a few chances, of course. but . . .

One of the two telephones rang in the office and Lawson hurried in, but Wykes had answered it. It was the ordinary telephone connected with the automatic exchange.

Wykes put down the receiver. He looked nervous. 'That was Sector B. They say your kid's just got away through a window.'

Lawson swore, stubbed out his cigarette, and thought. 'Tell them to carry on exactly as planned and check their watches. Fifteen minutes exactly to Strike.'

Did Keith know he was here – at the Site? No, he couldn't know, unless . . .

The second telephone buzzed. Lawson had kept this one hidden under a typewriter cover. It was a war-surplus field apparatus. A long wire was attached, ran discreetly through a hole bored in the floor, across the site workings and deep into the tunnel access to the bank vault – Sector C.

'What are you talking about?' demanded Lawson, irritably. 'Kids? *What* kids? Well, why ask me? Can't you blokes do anything without me nursing you? Grab 'em – and quick!'

He slammed down the receiver, pushed the instrument back under its cover, ignored an inquiring Wykes and went outside again. He lit another cigarette and watched the work going on out there, with eyes like glass.

Kids! Up here where you could see them were bad enough. But kids underground . . . how he loathed kids!

A shudder went right through him, like someone walking on his grave. Lawson knew this feeling. Last time he'd experienced it, quite like this, the judge had sent him down for seven long years . . .

He glanced across to the spot where Wykes's Jaguar, coated with dust from the site workings, stood with its bonnet facing the big gates. Well, if need be, he reckoned he could get a ton out of that on the coast road.

But the coast road made him think of the Isle of Wight again and he threw his cigarette away and called Ferdy and his companion across. 'Watch the wall,' he ordered. 'If my kid happens to show up, grab him and bring him to the office.'

13 Boy Aloft

To Bruce Roper, it seemed as if they had been down there for days: two pygmy earth-men condemned to burrow and scratch for ever in an alien world of darkness and distorted sound. Since first hearing the voices, they had stooped and crawled in every possible direction along several different sections of tunnel and piping. Least, Bruce assumed they were different, but sometimes he wondered whether, after all, they had merely got into a circular tube and were going round and round, like mice on an exercise wheel.

There were long silences, when the only sounds were their feet scraping over brick or metal and their breath panting closely in the confined space. Sometimes Sidney asked a shrill question which went on asking itself in a series of scaring echoes. Bruce shushed him but spoke gently, not wanting to frighten him. Pretend it was all a game of explorers – that was the best idea. If Sidney once cottoned-on to their plight and started bawling for keeps, his echoes would sound like a couple of jungles full of wild cats.

'Are we lost, Brucie?' (Ucie-ucie-ucie).

' – 'Course not, Sidney. Look, we'll just play a bit longer then we'll go out. Okay? You like being down here, don't you?'

'It's a bit scaring, Brucie!'

'Yeah, well ... it wouldn't be much fun if it weren't a *bit* scaring, would it, Sidney?'

Bruce felt his eardrums pounded by agitated air as some disturbance took place in the atmosphere around them. Then the tunnel shook and throbbed with the passage of an underground train. There was no kidding Sidney after that – he howled. But he was too frightened to make much noise: his pathetic little sobbings made eerie, mournful dissonances around them. Bruce stuck his fingers in his ears and gave them a wiggle to regain his hearing. A moment later he rather wished he hadn't.

The voices returned. They had crawled into a narrower tunnel than the other; a bent, twisted, ill-smelling brick trough, slimy to touch. Bruce thought he glimpsed a pin-point of light ahead, but it vanished at once. Then words wafted out of the renewed darkness: 'We'll get 'em. Hush! The knife ...'

'Poison-oison-oison ...'

'Nay, he come and we slit 'im!'

'Not slit 'im. Poison-oison-oison ...'

Least, that's what it sounded like to Bruce.

Sidney said, 'There's somebody along there, Brucie, but I can't see nuffink.'

Bruce hastily put a hand over Sidney's mouth, half smothering him. But for the first time their own movements and presence seemed to have communicated with whatever life existed at the end of the tunnel. There was the positive reaction of a caught breath, a poised tool. The mysterious light flashed on, then off again. The voices became secretive whispers and the first metallic foot-tread rang through the darkness.

Bruce crouched, holding Sidney behind him – still keeping a hand over his face. Poor Sidney was practically turning purple. At last, the new silence was broken by a more distinct clang of a

tool and somebody began whistling, very softly, through his
teeth. Bruce dragged Sidney on towards the sounds, rounded a
slight bend and saw whence the light, refracted by the curve of
the tunnel, had come.

A huge cavity had been rent in the brickwork of a thick wall:
Bruce could plainly see the ragged edge of freshly exposed
brick work, a pile of debris beside it and, illuminated by a
powerful arc lamp, two men at work with hand-drills and other
equipment.

Bruce waited to see no more though afterwards he remembered having seen other things: heavy canvas sacks, some elec-
trical gear, including a telephone ... but as he scrambled
back he had to let go of Sidney's mouth, and Sidney let forth.
His yelling wailed and whooped and all work ceased and the
light blinked out.

Then, in the dark, inviting silence that followed Bruce heard
two sounds: the cautious inquiring crunch of feet coming after
them and, less expected and more perplexing, the faint flutter
of something that sounded like bird's wings.

Beverley and Lena Chan were coming through Pimlico
from the newsagent's. Though they searched the streets on the
way they saw no sign of Angus. Neither he nor Bert Trunket
had been at home, and they hadn't confided in Mrs Trunket as
to what exactly they were up to. 'It must be something serious,
if those two are behaving like bosom pals!' she remarked.

The girls half walked and half ran as far as the Maybe Site.
They glanced up nervously at Big Annie's restless jib, then
hurried on towards Petty France. They turned into a cobbled
passage between the tall buildings because, Lena said, she remembered there was a telephone kiosk there and it was high
time they chanced a nine-nine-nine call.

It was half-way along this passage, close in to a set of railings, that they found Bruce and Sidney. Sidney was sitting on

the pavement, sobbing his heart out. As for Bruce, only his head, shoulders and arms were visible because he was stuck in a manhole. The manhole cover lay neatly beside him. Bruce was clutching Pigeon Henry in his hands. Bruce and Sidney both looked wild-eyed and pale, like things nurtured in pitch darkness.

'I've been trying to make Sidney fetch the police,' Bruce complained. 'But he won't budge. We've been down there for hours, and now we're being chased – I think . . .' He sounded terribly vague and dreamy. 'Cor! Give me a pull, will you? Sid, hold on to Henry . . . look out!'

Sidney dreamily reached for the pigeon, but it spread its dusty wings and flew out of his grasp.

'Oh, brilliant!' said Bruce.

'He'll come back,' said Lena. 'all the pigeons are heading back – we think. Can you sort of wriggle as we tug?'

'Can't you make yourself shrink a bit?' asked Beverley.

'Why don't they make these manholes wider, that's what I'd like to blooming know.'

'Sidney, you help,' said Beverley.

They all pulled. Bruce wriggled. He breathed in, then out. At last, red-faced and gasping for breath he sat on the pavement next to Sidney and said, 'Don't just stand there. Go and call the police. There's something going on – underground. There were these men, and a whacking great hole in a wall, and lights, and *crumbs* – the way they came after Sidney and me they weren't just workmen! One of 'em tried to sock us with a blooming great crow-bar and you know what we saw, too? Pound notes – *millions* of 'em!'

Five minutes before Strike, and Mousy Lawson came over the fence of the Maybe Site. He hadn't had far to come. He was a bit surprised when the two youths made for him and seized his arms, but he reckoned it was because they didn't know who he was. He tried to tell them, but they didn't take any notice – just led him across the rough ground to the office building. Lawson was alone in there and, at a glance from their boss, the youths withdrew.

Mousy looked at his father and something else puzzled him. It was as though he had been expected, and Lawson didn't look at all pleased to see him. Well, maybe it was the shock. He grinned wryly and said, 'You do recognize me, don't you?'

Lawson hadn't been sure how he would feel when he met his son face to face – if it happened. Now it had happened, and he knew what he felt: nothing. Nothing except irritation and anxiety that the seconds were ticking away and he had to do something that he hadn't time to bother with.

He said, 'You stupid young fool. It'll be Borstal for you next, d'you know that? You should have stayed at that kids' school where you had it nice and soft. Instead, you come tearing down here after me, and I must say you picked a dandy time. There's a job on. The balloon's due to go up at any moment.'

Mousy nodded. 'Yeah, I guessed.' His misgivings were too deep down for recognition; they made the ache in his stomach, the quickening of his heart-beat, but Mousy didn't know that. He could see that Lawson was angry. He thought it was the kind of anger that a parent feels when you have done something rash, and dangerous; but he's secretly on your side and presently his stern face will break into smiles and he'll chuck you under the chin and say it's okay, but don't do it again.

Mousy said, 'I'm not going to get in the way and nobody else knows I'm here. I wasn't mug enough to let myself be followed. It's the big time, isn't it? This job, I mean.'

Lawson didn't smile. His look was cold as he said, 'It's big all right.' But his mind was elsewhere. 'Who's this boy who's been sticking his nose in? He came here, asking a lot of questions . . . I hope he hasn't been chatting up the police. That was stupid, you know, getting a kid like that to run your errands, showing him the photo . . .'

So Chris *had* met his father, just as he had said. Mousy fought back the uneasiness that was creeping over him. 'Is that why you sent those monkeys in police uniforms after me? In case the kid called the real cops? I reckon I was a bit hasty, making a run for it.' Mousy shrugged, pretended he was more amused than anything else. 'I got mad because they were rough and I didn't know what was going on. It took me a while to figure why you'd played it that way – I should have known. That was smart . . .' But he couldn't seem to break this tension, bring any warmth or change to that cold stare. He went on babbling, not being able to bear the silence that fell whenever his words dried up. 'What about Audrey? Is she around? When do you reckon you'll get away? Is it going to be much trouble fixing it so's I come with you?'

Then Lawson said. 'You've got it all wrong, kid. We're not taking you anywhere. You must be dafter than I thought if you think that. Listen, for all you knew sticking your nose in my business might have put the kybosh on everything. If I had the time and thought it worth the bother I'd belt you so you'd never forget it . . .' There was a lot more; the names he called Keith, the jeering at all the trouble he'd gone to, admitting that the promises in the letter had been meant only to keep Keith quiet until Lawson and his new wife were safely abroad. And all the while he said these things, Mousy's dad kept his cold eyes fixed contemptuously on him. There was no outburst of anger; you couldn't say, well, he's blown his top and presently he'll say sorry, he didn't mean *that* . . .

Lawson meant it. This was the man Mousy had come to find, the man who had tried to make Chris shop him. And when Mousy had to face the truth at last, the truth was like sick in his throat. The hate, the anguish, the *knowing* – all spilled over and Mousy was through the door and racing across the sun-baked site, blindly making for the fence. Revenge clawed at his heart . . . he'd shop Lawson, he'd fix him, he'd bring the rozzers running . . .

Lawson's watchdogs saw him coming, got a signal from their master and advanced to cut Mousy off. Mousy was trapped. Half blind with tears, he knew there was no way out. But he ran on. He raced up the ladders of the scaffolding, and he didn't really know what he was doing. He was climbing up, up, up . . .

Angus was on his way to the Maybe Site. He no longer wore his uniform and this helped because nobody took any notice of him as he ran. He had most of the facts, now; facts, or intelligent guesses. He'd sorted a lot of it out with Bert Trunket and, before taking appropriate steps, intercepted some of Mrs Trunket's girls and boys on their way to dial nine-nine-nine at a telephone box.

But take what appropriate action you liked, Detective Constable Bert-cocky-Trunket wasn't going to get all the credit if Angus could help it! He couldn't help having wicked, wild, ambitious thoughts as he tried to make it to the Maybe Site before the 'cavalry' arrived. Och! if things worked out his way, he wouldn't only get a job with Scotland Yard; they'd practically award him the V.C.!

A hundred yards to go and Angus became aware of the crowds gathering at the fence. They were thickest at the locked gate, their faces turned skywards. What were they looking at – flying saucers?

Then Angus saw the dot on the scaffolding, High, high above the site, almost as far up as the giant jib of Big Annie. To Angus's sudden horror he realized that the swinging dot had what looked like waving arms – it was human!

'I'm a police officer. What's happened?'

A man in the crowd turned an ashen face in Angus's direction.

'Some harum-scarum shinned up the building. What we can't make out is where he came from and why he did it. Look at him – hanging by his braces, or something . . .'

'Isn't anything being done?' asked Angus.

'We dunno. It's up to them in the site, isn't it? We've been yelling blue murder, but they don't take any notice – won't even open the gate . . .'

Angus was over the gate in one powerful, well-coordinated movement. He didn't pay much attention to what was happening on the site – there was no time. A couple of workmen were part way up the scaffolding, hanging backwards, looking up at the frame of steel, hesitating whether to go further, awaiting some order that never came.

Angus didn't hesitate. He had heard enough to have a shrewd idea who the 'harum-scarum' was; not that it really made any difference. Whoever it had been up there, Angus would have done just what he was doing; he wasn't thinking or reasoning, any longer. He was acting at the behest of certain instincts.

His gaze was now fixed on the web of the steep scaffolding stretching up until it seemed to dissolve into the texture of a hair-net. For a while, he lost sight of the swinging dot as he made use of the tied ladders linking platform with platform. Then these ran out and he had to swing from bolted section to bolted section, hand over hand, legs wrapped round the smooth rods of the scaffolding.

Then he saw the boy – pretty close. He wasn't hanging by his braces; his plight was stranger than that. He had been carrying a haversack on his shoulder and it was the thick, khaki strap which had somehow become entangled with the bolted union securing a criss-cross of scaffolding tubes. The haversack had undoubtedly saved the boy's life, though he was swinging round and round in slow, helpless circles. His arms were pinioned by

the strap in such a way that he couldn't move them without a struggle, and a struggle would have been perilous.

'Don't move,' shouted Angus. Vaguely he became aware of happenings far down on the Maybe Site. He shot a quick glance down and almost paid for it; the scaffolding all around him seemed to sway. Before his giddiness passed off he clung still, watching the activities: men running like ants, a surge of move-men on the street side of the gate, a series of blue flashes from approaching vehicles.

Then he forced himself on and reached the bolts where Mousy Lawson's life hung in balance, above the far off wilder-ness of jagged stone and excavated workings. 'I'm going to grab you, laddie. You'll feel yourself swing in closer to the scaffolding. See if you can reach out and get a hold on some-thing – right?'

The fair head nodded. Angus made sure he had a bunch of the boy's clothing in his fist and drew him gently towards him. If the khaki strap slipped, he reckoned he could hold him for a few seconds at least . . .

But the strap held and Mousy, with most of his weight taken off the strap, was able to get a hand free and grasp the scaffolding, then find a foothold of his own. 'You can let go now, mate,' he said.

They sat side by side for a few moments with the high air whistling in their ears. Mousy was giving Angus a curious, unfriendly look. There were stains on his face – tear stains wondered Angus? And there was still chalk on his clothes, too – if it *was* chalk. 'Who are you, then?' Mousy asked. 'One of the gang down there?'

'I'm a copper,' said Angus, as though shy at admitting it.

The boy grinned. 'Oh, charming! This is it, then eh? You know who I am?'

'Yes,' said Angus. He suddenly thought of his crazy, am-bitious dream. There it goes, Angus, he thought. There goes your job with the C.I.D. Bert Trunket and the cavalry had got Lawson. All *he* had got was the Pimlico Pilferer.

For some reason, though, Angus felt happy – deep down happy.

14 Homers

The end was swift, conclusive, but not very tidy.

As soon as Keith Lawson had run berserk and climbed the scaffolding, and the crowd outside had come knocking like fate on the locked gate, Lawson knew the game was up.

But the plan he had worked out, though he'd admitted it was a little 'fancy', went on moving forward with the impetus of a well-greased road roller trundling down a slope.

So at Sector A (the Maybe Site) Big Annie actually picked up the crate containing canvas bags packed with currency notes from the deep tunnel access to the bank vaults, Sector C.

The tarpaulin-covered crate actually *was* lifted and sped across the blue sky, then dropped neatly enough into the fore-court of the disused garage in the condemned area behind the Site itself (Sector B). There the bogus policemen, safely (they thought) back from the 'arrest' of Mousy and only mildly alarmed at his escape, stacked the money rapidly but efficiently into the police van. The idea was that with the booty aboard it should sally forth into the streets of Pimlico, siren braying, blue light flashing, adding to the general confusion before heading discreetly to a secret rendezvous where the cargo could be transferred to a second and even more artfully disguised vehicle – a borrowed tanker, which would hold the coast road like a transcontinental express train.

Untidiest of all was the crowd from St. James's Park, led by a slightly dishevelled but still enthusiastic polka-dot girl. They had grown in size since the Chans had separated from them. They were still mostly children, but the crowd also included a number of sightseers who were young in heart, and needed to be, because the polka-dot girl was quite a firebrand.

They were decidedly untidy because they all had pigeons on the brain and couldn't be bothered with things like combs. They made a noisy, enthusiastic, untidy mob as they swept across Birdcage Walk, into Pimlico, and down towards the condemned buildings. Pigeons, apparently, had a penchant for insalubrious districts and rubbish heaps and broken windows; or perhaps they thought they would be safe from pursuit there.

They had reckoned without the polka-dot girl and her children, and child-like grown-ups. 'There goes the white one!' yelled the polka-dot girl. 'Through the alley.'

'I say,' complained a little-boy-fat-man. 'I really don't think it had a ring on its foot.'

'Oh, rubbish!' scolded the polka-dot girl. 'It has everything. Rings on its fingers, bells on its toes . . . come *on*!'

'I think I saw the cobbie,' cried a little-girl-old-lady. 'There – just going into . . . oh! he'll cut his feet on that *horrid* glass . . .'

Pigeon David, however, had more sense than to alight on the glass-studded wall. Pigeon David was awake; all Monsieur Poirot's pigeons seemed to be coming awake, and that made them even more difficult to catch than usual.

So the alley was full of people trying to catch pigeons, and that made it impossible for the police van to get out, unless it managed to fly over their heads.

Which of course it didn't. Least, not in time to avoid being blocked, at the end of the alley, by a police patrol car which planted itself at an untidy angle across the entrance . . .

At the Maybe Site, Wykes and Lawson, by a near-miracle, got the dusty Jag through the big gate, and it was purring nicely as it leaned round the corner smack, so to speak, in the arms of Bert Trunket and the 'cavalry' waiting in two other cars at the junction.

Bert Trunket presented his sardonic, Superintendent Barlow smile through the window, thinking that after this little lot he wouldn't be at all surprised if he got sergeant's stripes. Then he remembered that since he never wore a uniform the stripes wouldn't show, which was a pity . . .

Chris hadn't really expected to see Mousy again. But when it was all over, Angus found him wandering disconsolately towards the Poirots' house. Leo had gone ahead with Lena. They'd all watched the police close in on the Maybe Site area.

'I've been looking for you,' said Dickie Bird. 'And somebody else wants to see you.'

'Who's that?'

'Just tag along wi' me, laddie,' said Angus, and he took Chris to the police station.

He stopped outside one of the little closed rooms and placed a hand on Chris's shoulder. 'He's in there – the Pilferer. Take it easy, Chris. Just let him do the talking, if he wants.'

'Is he . . . all right?'

'He'll do. He's been through a lot, but he's tough – in more ways than one. He's a great talker, isn't he? I don't think he's stopped since we brought him in. But for all his bragging and nonsense, you know what I think?' Angus tried to think of the right way to put it. 'Aye, inside the big tough guy there's a wee laddie – maybe even a guid laddie – trying to get out.'

'What's going to happen to him. Mr Dickie?'

'Now, you mean? Weel, he'll be sent back to Bristol, of course. They won't be too hard on him in the circumstances ...'

'No,' said Chris. 'I mean, later ... in the *end*.'

'Och! who are we to guess at the end of a boy – or a man? Maybe Keith Lawson has learned something today. He's had a few hard lessons ...' Angus wearily turned the handle of the door. 'Perhaps he's learned, Chris, but it isn't only the Lawsons of this world who need a powerful lot of teaching ...'

They went in. Mousy looked up cheerfully. They'd fed him and let him wash himself and given him a bundle of comics to look at.

He grinned. 'Watcher, bonzo!'

'Hi, Mousy.'

Mousy was staring at Chris's face. 'Blimey, that's quite a shiner you've got there, mate!' He didn't apologize for Chris's black eye. 'Hey, they reckon you've been sticking your neck out, not letting on where I was.'

'Yeah.' Chris felt uncomfortable. Was Mousy going to try and thank him for something? He didn't deserve any thanks – not the way things had worked out. Anyway, he needn't have worried!

'I reckon they'll chuck the book at you, mate, then they'll perhaps send you over to Bristol along with me. That'd be a giggle, wouldn't it? I hope you can play ping-pong!'

Chris didn't know what to say, so he said, 'You know we thought some old lady lived in that house – over the basement? Well, it was an old man – in a pinny.'

Mousy thought that was funny. He guffawed. Then his expression changed, several times. He said, 'You know that old moggy at the basement? Reckon it was a stray?'

'I don't know, Mousy.'

'Well, do us a favour and find out if you can. He ought to be looked after.'

'Okay, Mousy.'
'Ta-ta, then. Don't do anything I wouldn't do!'
And that was all.

It was evening at last. Some of the brightness had gone from the sky and a sweet breeze wafted in from the lung of the river. The streets of Pimlico were practically deserted again, and over the Maybe Site Big Annie brooded tall and melancholy.

Bruce and Sidney had just collected their basket from the underground station. Now they thumped rhythmically along, not talking at first.

Then Sidney suddenly shouted, 'I was scared down there, Brucie. It was scary, wasn't it?'

'Yeah, a bit, Sid,' agreed Bruce.

'I bet you wasn't really scared though, was you Brucie? You wasn't scared because you're big. When I'm big, like you, I won't be scared will I, Brucie?'

'Yeah. I mean, no – not so much,' said Bruce. He was really thinking of pigeons. He was wondering about pigeons. As they neared the Poirots' house he made Sidney hurry a bit. 'Come on, Sid. We've got to hurry.'

They were all at the lofts: Chris, Beverley, the Chans, the younger children, the puppy.

But no fly-away pigeons. Not one.

The children had managed to placate angry and anxious parents. They'd eaten dinners and teas all in one. They'd heard about the crime from Angus – the bits they hadn't known before. But now they weren't thinking about crime.

They were thinking about pigeons.

'They can't be far away,' said Leo. 'The girl from the park, and the crowd – they came right into Pimlico. That's how they helped catch the police van.'

'And after that,' moaned Lena Chan, 'they forgot all about pigeons. They were much more interested in the robbery.'

'Well, you couldn't *blame* them,' said Leo.

'I blooming do!' grumbled Bruce. He looked up at the vacant racing loft. The traps hung open like mouths, yawning -- or laughing. 'They probably scared them. All that yelling and ...'

'Listen!' said Lena Chan.

They listened. They couldn't believe it, at first. There was a faint fluttering, breathy sound – like the fall of leaves, or ... the whisper of wings in the sky.

Their faces all turned up. Now, against the egg-blue sky, they could make out the shapes of flying birds, their wings made silver and gold as the sinking sun struck them.

The pigeons! They had all come together, all six, and were flying round and round the rooftops making a tighter and brighter halo of feathers as they prepared to descend to the loft.

Pigeon George and Pigeon Freddy, the gay pieds – they were first in. Then came Pigeon Oswald and Pigeon Egbert, the albinos. They were a little slower. Pigeon Henry the chequered, was slower and later still, but last of all came the little cobbie, Pigeon David. He *was* late. But it didn't matter, because he was home.

All the pigeons had flown home.

M Books is a series consisting of some of the best contemporary fiction for young people. Other books you may enjoy are:

The Runaway Summer Nina Bawden
Tales of a Fourth-Grade Nothing Judy Blume
The Day of the Pigeons Roy Brown
The Eighteenth Emergency Betsy Byars
The Pinballs Betsy Byars
After the Goat Man Betsy Byars
The Cartoonist Betsy Byars
The TV Kid Betsy Byars
The Night Swimmers Betsy Byars
Time Trap Nicholas Fisk
Trillions Nicholas Fisk
Elidor Alan Garner
My Side of the Mountain Jean George
I Am David Anne Holm
The Jungle Book Rudyard Kipling
Just So Stories Rudyard Kipling
The Battle of Bubble and Squeak Philippa Pearce
The Shadow Cage Philippa Pearce
The Cats Joan Phipson
Dragon Slayer Rosemary Sutcliff
Sun Horse, Moon Horse Rosemary Sutcliff
Horned Helmet Henry Treece
Charlotte's Web E B White
The Crane Reiner Zimnik